NEW BEGINNINGS BOOK 2: THE HARVEST BALL

A PRIDE AND PREJUDICE VARIATION

LILY BERNARD

❀ Created with Vellum

DEDICATION

For Cele Axelrod: the woman who taught me to love books and demonstrated to me, and so many others, the many gifts of reading. I love her without measure and I am forever in her debt.

SYNOPSIS: NEW BEGINNINGS BOOK ONE

New Beginnings - Book Two: The Harvest Ball, is a stand-alone novel; however, the author is happy to include a synopsis of Book One. Enjoy! LB

SYNOPSIS
NEW BEGINNINGS BOOK ONE: WICKHAM'S REVENGE

This story is a captivating variation of Jane Austen's Pride and Prejudice. In the winter of 1811, George Wickham traveled to Pemberley to ask Fitzwilliam Darcy for money. He needed to flee from England and escape his mounds of unpaid gambling debts. Upon arriving at his childhood home, he learned that Darcy was not in Derbyshire and while he awaited his return, Wickham seduced Nora Kelly, one of Pemberley's young maids. As he got to know Nora better, he fell in love with her and they were secretly betrothed. Darcy did not return to Derbyshire and

Wickham left for London, hoping to earn enough money to marry Nora. Shortly after his departure, Nora realized she was carrying Wickham's child.

Nora had no way to tell Wickham about the baby and when her condition became obvious, she was sent to the Darcy estate in Scotland to await the birth. A terrible carriage accident on the road north claimed Nora's life and that of her unborn child. After he had won enough money at London's seediest gambling halls, Wickham returned to Pemberley to marry Nora and learned that she and their baby were dead. Wickham blamed Darcy for their deaths and swore revenge on him and everyone he loved. Darcy was unaware of any of the events that had transpired at Pemberley in his absence. He was in Hertfordshire helping Charles Bingley learn about managing Netherfield Park.

After the Meryton Assembly, Darcy and Elizabeth met while walking near Oakham Mount. They enjoyed their first conversation together and met again and again to talk. No one else was aware that over the course of several months of getting to know each other, they fell in love; Darcy proposed, and Elizabeth happily accepted. Before reaching Longbourn to ask for Mr. Bennet's permission, Darcy received an express from Colonel Fitzwilliam. Darcy told Elizabeth that he had been called away by a family emergency. He did not wish to frighten her with the truth; he had to leave Hertfordshire immediately in order to rescue his sister. Georgiana Darcy was being held for ransom in Ramsgate by his childhood friend turned mortal enemy, George Wickham.

In the mayhem surrounding Georgiana's rescue, Darcy was mercilessly stabbed in the back by Wickham. The assailant, as well as some of his men, escaped capture while everyone was busy trying to save Darcy's life. In order to satisfy Wickham's quest for revenge and eliminate the threat to Darcy's loved ones, the world at large was informed that Darcy had died by Wickham's hand.

A critically injured Darcy was brought to Scotland to begin a months' long recovery. On the road to Ramsgate, Darcy had told Richard about his betrothal and after bringing his cousin to Scotland, he went to Longbourn and told Elizabeth the heartbreaking news. Darcy never had the opportunity to ask for her father's permission, as such, they were not officially engaged. Elizabeth cried alone every night; all her dreams of the life she was looking forward to sharing with Darcy had been shattered.

Eventually, Elizabeth told her father everything and after months of watching his favorite daughter's lingering melancholy, he suggested that she might benefit from a change of scenery. Although Elizabeth continued to mourn William's death, she agreed to take her father's advice. She moved to Derbyshire to live with Jane and Charles Bingley at their new estate, Birchwood Manor.

After escaping from Ramsgate, George Wickham

resumed his degenerate habits in London. Many months after he believed he had killed Darcy, Wickham was shot by a fellow gambler to whom Wickham owed a great deal of money. Richard Fitzwilliam wrote to Darcy in Scotland to inform him of Wickham's death. He told his cousin that when he was well enough to travel, it would be safe for him to return to England.

A year had passed since Darcy and Elizabeth had fallen in love. She still thought about Darcy every day, but she knew it was time to move forward with her life. After living with the Bingleys for several months, Elizabeth was introduced to Lord Winthrope, one of the Bingley's neighbors. She came to enjoy spending time with 'Brooks' and eventually accepted his proposal. Almost a year after she learned of his demise, the "dead" Mr. Darcy walked into the Bingleys' drawing room. Expecting to reunite with his fiancée, Elizabeth was forced to choose between her two suitors. There can be no doubt that Elizabeth and Darcy were reunited and eventually married. At the end of Book One in July 1813, the Darcys had been married for almost a year and Elizabeth had just told her husband that they were going to be parents.

CHAPTER 1

AUGUST 1, 1813

After being the magistrate in Lambton for more than fifteen years, Josiah Harris prided himself as being a good judge of people. He often told his friends that he could spot unsavory characters on sight. After university, he studied the law, but preferred his role in helping to maintain a peaceful way of life for the area residents of Lambton more than he had being a barrister. The owners of some of the larger estates near Lambton were wise enough to employ security men to protect themselves from the criminals who viewed their homes as targets. Other property owners, who operated their estates with minimal staff when they were not in residence, were more subject to being robbed and made his job more difficult.

The largest property near Lambton, and in all of Derbyshire, was Pemberley, the Darcy family's home for more than two hundred years. Mr. Harris knew that Mr. Darcy was very protective of his family, his property and his staff and maintained a high level of security whether or not the family was in residence.

Late one afternoon, Mr. Harris was leaving his office when he noticed four filthy, slovenly dressed men riding through Lambton. Their clothes were dirty and torn, and their boots were caked with mud. There was something about the men that made the hair on the back of Josiah's neck stand on end. The men were not clean shaven, and they looked as if they had not bathed in months. None of the men bothered to look his way and he thought it was odd that they did not tip their hats or acknowledge him in any way. One man, in particular, with very long, dirty dark hair, inky black eyes and an untrimmed beard, stayed in his mind as he walked toward his carriage to make his way home. *I hope those men are just passing through town. If they remain in Lambton, I will have to keep my eyes out for them. Looks to me like they may be up to no good, but I hope they take their trouble elsewhere. In the morning, I will speak to all the shopkeepers and stable hands and perhaps I should send a note to the local property owners. There was something not right about those men. Time will tell if my intuition is correct.*

SEVERAL WEEKS LATER, REBECCA REYNOLDS WALKED along the upstairs hallway and took a moment to glance out the window. She observed the happy couple who resided at Pemberley walking toward one of the many scenic paths surrounding the estate. For a few moments, she smiled as she followed Mr. and Mrs. Darcy's progress as they strolled arm in arm in the late August afternoon sun. *What a handsome couple they make! He is so tall and muscular, and she is such a petite woman with beautiful dark curly hair which is always escaping from her bonnet! When she stands beside him, he towers over her. I am so happy Fitzwilliam made a love match. All the times Miss Bingley was a guest here, I was afraid she would try to compromise my master and force him to marry her. She never had a kind word to say to anyone and I never cared for that shrewish woman!*

Things have turned out quite well for the man I have known since he was just a small boy. Soon there will be a new baby in the Pemberley nursery –time has passed so quickly! In the short time they have been married, Mrs. Darcy's presence has transformed Pemberley into a home that is filled with love, laughter and joy. I have been the housekeeper here for more than twenty-five years and I cannot remember a time when Pemberley was a happier place to work. I must get back to my responsibilities; I will go down to the kitchen and make sure everything is being readied for dinner this evening.

"Elizabeth, please take my arm. The ground here is quite uneven."

"With pleasure, sir. Where are we going today?" She was enjoying being shown another one of the many picturesque walking paths around Pemberley that she had not yet traversed. The beautiful landscape surrounding her home brought her endless joy. Although quite different from the lands surrounding Longbourn, her childhood home, Elizabeth came to embrace the dense forests and colder climate than she was accustomed to when she was living in Hertfordshire.

She never dreamed she would ever feel the happiness her marriage to this wonderful man brought her. All the months she thought her beloved William was dead by Wickham's hand, she was certain she could never feel joy again. She looked up and admired the leaves on the trees along their path. Every day, they changed a little more from dark green to magnificent shades of red and yellow.

"You will find out soon enough," he responded playfully. They walked slowly, mindful of the uneven path. "What I am about to show you was very special to me and Richard when we were boys."

"Now, I am even more eager to get there."

"Patience, my love, patience." They continued walking for several more minutes until Darcy stopped. He pointed to a large tree in the distance which looked as if it had been split in half by lightning many years ago. "If you can find this old burnt out tree, you will know where Richard and I hid when we were young." Elizabeth looked around for anything that could be used as a hiding place and unable to do so, she was becoming more and more curious about their destination.

He led his wife past the landmark tree and stopped when they stood in front of a row of very tall bushes which were growing close together. Darcy took Elizabeth's hand and led her around the dense vegetation to where they both saw a large rock formation with a wide opening. "It is a cave! What a wonderful hiding place! No one could ever find it if they had not been here before. Those shrubs protect the opening from being seen by anyone walking by."

"Richard and I often hid here when imaginary pirates were chasing us." Darcy laughed reminiscing about his youth, "or when we were in trouble and did not want my tutor to find us. As you can see it is not very large, so we stopped hiding here when we had both grown too big to fit inside!" They shared a smile thinking about the silly misadventures of two young boys.

"Thank you for showing me your cave. It is the perfect place to hide!" She rubbed her growing belly and asked, "will you show our little babe your secret hiding place?"

"I will be happy to, then we will know where our child is hiding!"

"I suppose that our little one will find his own places to hide from us!" They laughed and began to walk back toward the manor house.

"There is something I need to speak with you about."

"Is anything wrong?"

"No, all is well. It is just that now we are nearing the end of the growing season, the tenants are getting ready for the harvest and I will not be able to spend so much time with you every day. I need to help Bethel oversee the harvesting and storage of the crops. You must agree that you will not walk any farther than the formal gardens near the house on your own. In fact, you have probably noticed that we have taken on two new footmen, a Mr. Sanders and a Mr. Johnson; someone should always be available to escort you. I cannot fulfill my responsibilities to Pemberley if I am worried about you walking about unescorted." Darcy paused and took his wife's hands and placed them over his heart. "I love you and our little babe too much to allow anything that could possibly harm you to occur. Will you promise to agree? I am serious, and I must have your cooperation."

"I understand, and I promise you that I will not venture out without one of the footmen escorting me. Are you happy now?"

He took his wife into his arms and embraced her. "I am happier now than I ever dreamed I could be. You and the baby are the most important things in my life and I will do everything in my power to keep you both safe."

Elizabeth reached up and placed her gloved hand on his face. "I will never do anything to risk our health and I promise you that I will not go walking without an escort. Does that please you, my husband?"

Darcy raised her hand to his lips, "yes, I am pleased. Let us return to the house; it is time you had something to eat and then you can rest."

"I am feeling a bit hungry. I hope I do not continue to increase at this rapid rate or by the time our child is born, I will not be able to climb the stairs to our chambers."

"If that should occur, I will happily make up one of the downstairs rooms as our bed chamber or I will carry you up the stairs whenever you wish." Darcy and Elizabeth were smiling when they entered Pemberley; they were both happy and looking forward to the future.

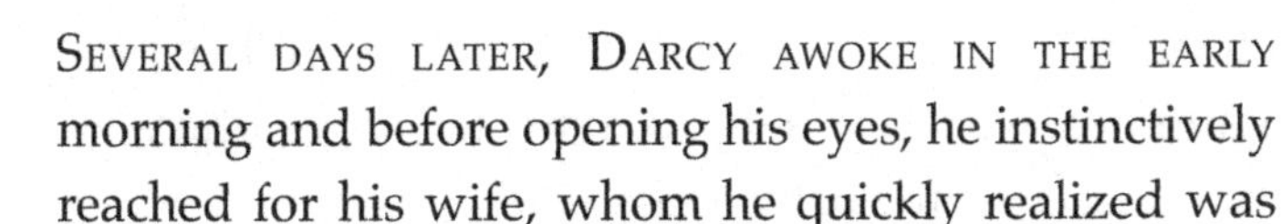

Several days later, Darcy awoke in the early morning and before opening his eyes, he instinctively reached for his wife, whom he quickly realized was not in bed. He opened his eyes and when he sat up he saw that the doors to their balcony were opened; the sheer curtains that hung on either side of the doorway were stirring in the morning breeze. He slipped his banyan over his head and quietly walked to the doorway where he saw his beautiful wife standing on the balcony; her long chestnut curls were moving in the gentle breeze. She was looking out at Pemberley's lake, which was still shrouded in early morning mist. He came up behind his wife and placed his hands on her stomach and bent to kiss her neck. Elizabeth leaned back against her husband enjoying the feeling of his arms around her. They stood in silence until Darcy suddenly said, "I just felt the baby move!"

"Yes, our little one is very active. The baby moving so much is why I have trouble sleeping. Give me your hand again if you would like to feel your child kicking his Mama."

He gave her his hand and she placed it on the side of her baby bump. A few moments later, when he again felt his child moving, he looked at his beloved wife with tears in his eyes. "Does it hurt you when the babe moves like that?" She smiled and shook her head. "I never imagined what it must feel like for you. I love you so much," he leaned over and kissed the spot on his wife's belly where he had just felt his child moving, "and our little babe. When Mr. Laurence was last here, did he tell you when we should expect the baby to arrive?"

"Around the end of October or the beginning of November, many weeks before Christmas."

"The baby will be the best Christmas gift either of us has ever received."

"I hope I am recovered from the birth well before everyone arrives for the Christmas holidays."

"Would you like your mother to be here for your confinement?" Darcy asked with trepidation. He was fond of Mrs. Bennet and that fondness was enhanced by the many miles between Pemberley and Longbourn.

"I want Jane to be with me when the time comes for the baby to be born. Perhaps I should write to Mama and tell her that the babe is expected about the time my family will arrive for Christmas."

"I will not argue with you about *that* decision, but I just do not want you taking on too much by entertaining everyone so soon after the baby is born. And shortly after the new year we will leave for London for Georgiana's first Season."

"That is why I am so happy that Mrs. Reynolds and the rest of the staff are so efficient. The Darcy House staff will help me prepare for Georgiana's coming out Ball. I am sure Aunt Patricia will be unable to resist helping plan her niece's debut into London society. She has two sons and our sister is the closest thing she has to a daughter. I plan to rely on her expertise as much as she will allow."

"I suppose if you are still indisposed, there are others who can help out. I think we should discuss this topic further but for now…" Darcy took his wife into his arms, began kissing her and they soon forgot about discussing anything else.

LATER THAT MORNING, THEY WERE SITTING AT BREAKFAST before he had to leave with their steward. He looked up from the correspondence he was reading, "I have received a note from Mr. Carter, the new vicar in Kympton. He asked me if we could help some of his most needy parishioners."

"I hope you will tell him that he can count on our support. Are you pleased with your decision to give the living to Mr. Carter?"

"Yes, very much so. Although he is on the young side, he came with very good references and he appears to exude a kind of inner peace. Young men like Carter are very rare indeed. He comes from a very wealthy family who made their money in trade; as a second son he will not take over his family's business. Mr. Carter said that he always felt a calling to the Church.

"Shall we invite him to the Harvest Ball? We can get to know him better and he will have an opportunity to meet some of his flock outside of the church walls."

"That is an excellent idea, my dear. I will add him to our invitation list, but for now, I must depart. I hate to leave you after such a lovely morning, but I am sure Bethel is waiting impatiently for me at the stables." Darcy kissed Elizabeth's forehead and left her to finish her breakfast in the small family dining room.

Later that morning, when she returned from her walk around Pemberley's beautiful gardens, Mrs. Reynolds approached her. "Mrs. Darcy, I was wondering if you have time today for us to discuss some plans for the Harvest Ball?"

"Of course, Mrs. Reynolds, I am eagerly looking forward to the party. Mr. Darcy told me that Pemberley has not hosted the event for many years. I believe all the tenants and staff are looking forward to it."

"Indeed, they are, ma'am."

"I will change my dress and meet you in my sitting room in twenty minutes."

"Thank you, madam."

TWENTY MINUTES LATER, WHEN MRS. REYNOLDS JOINED

her mistress, she was carrying a large sheath of papers. "What is all that?"

"These are all the notes I could find on planning a Harvest Ball. Some of them go all the way back to well before I came to Pemberley."

"Let us each take a handful and see if we can glean any good ideas from them. I would like to make this year's Harvest Ball the best one Pemberley has ever held." Both women smiled and got down to work. They looked through the many sheets of notes for ideas about décor, refreshments, music and the guest list. When they came across an idea they liked, they shared their thoughts and Mrs. Reynolds wrote down their decisions. When they were finished, Elizabeth was quite tired and hungry and asked the housekeeper if it was time for lunch.

"Yes, madam, luncheon will be served as soon as you are ready."

"I am feeling a bit tired right now. I believe I will rest a few minutes in my chambers and then I will ring when I would like my lunch."

"Of course, just let me know when you are ready. I would be happy to have a tray brought up to your sitting room if you would rather not dine downstairs."

"Thank you, bringing a tray to my sitting room is a good idea."

CHAPTER 2

When Darcy returned home in the late afternoon, he could not find his wife in any of the downstairs rooms. He saw Mrs. Reynolds walking toward him and asked her if she knew where Mrs. Darcy was. "I believe she may still be up in her chambers. After her morning walk, we worked for several hours on the plans for the Harvest Ball. When we were finished, she mentioned she was tired and asked that a lunch tray be brought up to her sitting room."

"Thank you, I will look for her there." He bounded up the steps of Pemberley's grand staircase and walked toward his chambers. He changed out of his soiled clothes before he continued to search for his wife. A few minutes later, Darcy entered the sitting room between their adjoining suites and noticed that the food on the tray had not been touched. He tried not to be alarmed as he quietly entered his wife's bed chamber. He saw her sleeping in her clothes and shoes on top of the counterpane. As he quickly walked to his wife, a feeling of panic rose in his chest. *If anything has happened to her, I do not know if I can continue to live; she is my heart and soul.* Darcy sat down on the edge of the bed and his weight on the mattress caused Elizabeth to stir and she slowly opened her eyes. He gently swept some of her curls from her face, "my love, are you well? You have been sleeping for a long time."

"William," she said groggily as he helped her sit up. "I was so tired after my meeting with Mrs. Reynolds. All I wanted to do was rest for a few minutes before lunch. What time is it?"

"It is well after four. Are you certain you feel well? Shall I send for Mr. Laurence?"

"I do not need a doctor but now that I am awake, I am feeling hungry. I do not remember eating lunch."

"The lunch tray in your sitting room was untouched."

"Will you join me for some refreshments and a cup of tea?"

He nodded in agreement. "Let me find Hannah and then I will help you out of bed."

When he entered the hallway, Darcy saw Elizabeth's maid coming toward his wife's chambers carrying some fresh linen. He requested that food be sent up to their sitting room and asked that Mr. Laurence be summoned as quickly as possible. Darcy returned to his wife's chambers and helped her as she tried to fix her hair and straighten her skirts after sleeping so long in her clothes.

Elizabeth held on to her husband's arm as they slowly walked into their sitting room. A few minutes later, their food arrived and they were both quite hungry. Before they were completely finished with their repast, Hannah announced that Mr. Laurence had arrived.

Elizabeth looked at her husband with feigned anger. "I told you that I did not need the doctor."

"I know, but I was worried about you sleeping so long today. I just want to hear Mr. Laurence tell us that all is well."

"I will allow Mr. Laurence to examine me and when he is finished, I am sure he will tell you that you are worried for no reason."

While Elizabeth was being seen by the doctor, Darcy was unable to sit down and paced back and forth in the sitting room,. He could not stop thinking that giving birth to his sister had led to the untimely death of his mother. After Mr. Laurence had finished his examination, Hannah helped Elizabeth get dressed and the doctor opened the door to the sitting room and asked Darcy to join them.

"Sir, your wife is absolutely fine. Her fatigue is quite normal for a woman in the final months of carrying a child. She told me that she often has trouble sleeping at night because the baby's movements are keeping her awake. Her irregular nighttime sleep is likely the cause of the long nap today. You should not be surprised if the fatigue increases until your child is born. Please summon me if you think anything unusual is happening. The baby is growing nicely and should arrive by the end of October. Mrs. Darcy must eat well; continue her moderate exercise and a daily rest should see her through to the birth of a healthy baby."

"Thank you, Mr. Laurence. I told my husband there was nothing to worry about."

"I will see Mr. Laurence out and then return to you. Since you are so tired, would you like to have dinner in our sitting room tonight?"

"I think that is a lovely idea."

When the two men stood by the front door, Mr. Laurence turned to Darcy. "I did not wish to alarm your wife, but I noticed that her ankles are a bit swollen. That could mean absolutely nothing, or it could be an indication that she is developing a more dangerous condition. My best advice is to watch her carefully and make sure she sits with her legs elevated whenever possible. I will return in two days and we should know more by then. Please try not to worry, your wife is a very healthy young woman and she and the baby will be fine. Good day, sir."

"Thank you for coming so quickly Mr. Laurence." As soon as the doctor had departed, Mrs. Reynolds walked toward Darcy.

"Sir, I overheard what Mr. Laurence said about Mrs. Darcy, and I will make sure that his orders are followed. We are all very fond of the mistress and will do anything to accommodate her needs."

"Thank you, I do not know what we would do without you. I know you will instruct the staff on what needs to be done. I am trying not to worry, but you know the basis of my concern."

"Indeed, I do. You would do well to remember that Mrs. Darcy is much healthier and far more active than your dear mother. I am sure she will easily bring your child into this world and probably go for a five mile walk the next day." Mrs. Reynolds smiled at the man she had known since he was a boy. She placed her hand on his arm and gave him a reassuring squeeze, "worry not, all will be well."

Darcy smiled at the woman who was so much more than Pemberley's housekeeper and placed his hand briefly over hers. "Thank you for your comforting words." He climbed the stairs and returned to their sitting room where he found Elizabeth reading a book. "How are you feeling now, my love?"

"I feel refreshed by my nap and the food, but I am still a bit fatigued. I like the idea of having dinner sent up tonight...if that is still agreeable to you."

"More than agreeable. However, Mr. Laurence just told me that when you are sitting, you should keep your feet elevated." He quickly glanced around the room and spotted an ottoman near the fireplace. He did not want to wait for a footman to help him and quickly brought it over to her and kneeled at her feet. He took both her legs and placed them atop the soft foot rest.

"Seeing you kneeling before me like that, I thought you might be trying to propose again," Elizabeth teased. "In fact, I do not remember you kneeling when you proposed to me on the terrace at Birchwood Manor."

"I am so grateful every day that you are my wife. If you would like me to propose to you from this, or any other position, I will most happily comply," Darcy responded trying to keep his voice from reflecting his concern for his wife's health.

She smiled and looked into the eyes of her husband. "I do not believe that will be necessary and besides, you do not look very comfortable right now. Will you not sit next to me while I read? Or better still, will you read to me? You know how I love to hear the sound of your voice." Darcy sat beside Elizabeth and began to read aloud from the book of poetry she had been holding. He placed his arm around her shoulder and she very happily leaned into his chest as she listened to his beautiful voice reading some love poems by William Blake.

Before they realized how much time had passed, several maids began bringing in their dinner trays. They both sat up from the position of comfort they found in each other's arms. "Do I need to keep my feet elevated while I eat?"

"I believe the doctor was very explicit. Your feet are to be elevated whenever possible. I will be happy to prepare a plate for you so there is no need for you to get up."

Elizabeth was not happy about her husband's edict but decided to relax and enjoy being so well cared for. After she told him which foods she wished to eat, he brought the plate, cutlery and napkin to where she was sitting. When her husband attempted to feed her, she had had enough. "William, I am not an invalid! I will sit here with my feet up on the ottoman, but I refuse to be spoon fed!"

"I apologize if I went too far; you know I would do anything in my power to help you."

"You are forgiven, and I love how you wish to care for me but there has to be a limit. Please, make yourself a plate and join me."

ELIZABETH WAS STILL TIRED DESPITE HER NAP. SHE HAD

been awake most of the night due to the baby's kicking. Darcy was tired after a day of riding from farm to farm and helping out wherever an extra pair of hands were needed. Shortly after finishing their dinner they decided to retire for the night. When they got into bed, she turned her back to her husband and he reached over her hip and placed his hand on her large stomach. "Elizabeth, please do not be angry with me for summoning Mr. Laurence. You and the baby are my only concern. If necessary, I will stay at home and look after you and Bethel can handle the harvest on his own. Would you like that?"

Elizabeth slowly rolled over to speak to her husband face to face. "You, more than anyone else, know how independent I have always been." She began to cry. "I am not angry with you. How could I be when your only concern is for my well-being? In truth, I am angry with myself. I behaved like the same foolish girl I was in Hertfordshire where I could walk as far as I wanted. I know I walked too far earlier today and then I had a long meeting with Mrs. Reynolds. I realize that I have been very selfish. You have responsibilities to Pemberley and our tenants and Mr. Bethel." Darcy dried her tears as she caressed his face. "I promise that my only responsibility will be to take care of myself and the baby. Although, I still do not think it is necessary for you to feed me, I will follow the doctor's orders and keep my feet up as much as I can. Now kiss me goodnight, I believe I heard Mr. Laurence order me to fall asleep in the arms of the man I love. I am very happy to follow *those* doctor's orders and get plenty of rest."

He was eager to comply and gently kissed his wife. A few moments later, he could hear the sweet sound of his wife sleeping. Darcy believed what Elizabeth said about following the doctor's orders, but he would worry until Mr. Laurence returned in a few days to see if she was in any danger.

THE DOCTOR RETURNED TO PEMBERLEY IN TWO DAYS' time. After he examined Elizabeth, he told her that she and the baby were quite well and that the swelling around her ankles had decreased. "I still believe that it is a good idea to keep your legs elevated whenever convenient. You should continue your daily walks, but you must not walk too long or walk alone. If anything unusual occurs, please do not hesitate to summon me."

"Thank you, Mr. Laurence, I will be happy to convey your instructions to Mr. Darcy."

IT HAD BEEN SEVERAL WEEKS SINCE THE DAY DARCY HAD shown Elizabeth his childhood hideaway and, once again, he left the house directly after breakfast to supervise the harvest with their steward. After finishing her meal, Elizabeth left the manor house accompanied by Mr. Sanders, one of the new footmen. As they were walking past the stables on their way to one of the walking paths, Sanders hesitated before asking, "Pray excuse me ma'am, but as this is the first time I am escorting you, how close do you wish me to walk?"

"I do not believe there is any reason for you to stay too close, but for safety's sake, you should always keep me in sight."

"Yes, madam, I understand. Please lead the way." Elizabeth began a slow walk along one of Pemberley's more scenic paths, although with the advent of autumn, every day the path was covered with more and more multi-colored fallen leaves. She walked for about an hour and then returned to the house for lunch and a rest.

CHAPTER 3

The following afternoon, Darcy returned home from supervising the harvest and was happily surprised to find his cousin, Richard Fitzwilliam, awaiting him in his study. "What a wonderful surprise! Why did you not let us know you were coming?"

"Darcy, I am here to speak to you about a very serious matter. I have not yet seen your lovely wife, and you should decide if you will want her to know what I am about to tell you."

"Richard, you are frightening me. What has happened that is so serious that you travelled here all the way from Kent? If it could not be put in a letter, it must be a very grave matter, indeed."

"I came in person because I wish to help you eliminate the danger your family is now facing."

"Please continue. I am always happy for your

assistance, but I do not know what kind of danger you believe we are facing. I have not received any messages from Mr. Harris warning us of any danger."

"Harris would have no knowledge of what I am about to tell you. Some of the Bow Street Runners who helped us recover Georgiana, have written to me. It seems that several of Wickham's men who escaped capture in Ramsgate two years ago, have been seen in Derbyshire."

Darcy jumped up from his chair. "What are you saying? Where are they? We must find them today!"

"Think about what you are saying. These men are all lifelong criminals know how to hide. Wickham never got his hands on Georgiana's dowry and he never paid any of them a farthing. The Runners believe that Wickham's men are desperate and may still try to harm your family in some plan to make money. I would suggest you accompany your wife and sister whenever they leave the house. Perhaps it would be wise if you hire a few more guards, armed guards."

"Is the situation so serious that Pemberley needs to become an armed fortress in order to protect my family?"

"These men thought they were going to make a great deal of money helping Wickham kidnap your sister. I have no doubt that they would abduct any member of your household and hold them for a very high ransom. The armed guards would only be here until the danger has passed."

"Georgiana is currently visiting your parents at Matlock Manor, but I will write to your father and tell him to be more vigilant. I will also send extra guards to protect my sister on her journey back to Pemberley."

"That sounds like an excellent idea. What about protecting Lizzy on her daily rambles?"

"That has already been taken care of; she no longer walks out alone, she is always accompanied by a servant or me. I just hired two new footmen to ensure someone is always available to escort her while I am with my steward. Richard, she should be made aware of this new threat. I will ask her to join us here, so we can both speak to her."

Darcy rang for his housekeeper and after she entered her master's study, "Mrs. Reynolds, would you ask Mrs. Darcy to join us?"

"Of course, sir."

Several minutes later, the housekeeper returned to her master's study. "I am sorry, sir, but it seems that Mrs. Darcy has not yet returned from her walk."

Darcy tried to control the panic in his voice; he knew his wife preferred to walk in the morning and it was already late afternoon. "What time did she leave the house?"

"She and Sanders left shortly after breakfast. Neither has returned."

"It is almost four o'clock!" Darcy was truly worried now. "Where could she be? Richard, ride out with me and help me find her and the footman. If any harm has come to my wife or our baby, I swear I will kill all of Wickham's men with my bare hands!" He tried to calm himself before asking, "Mrs. Reynolds, will you direct some of the footmen and groundskeepers to start searching the walking paths on foot?"

"Of course, Mr. Darcy. I am terribly sorry I did not realize how long Mrs. Darcy had been gone. I have been in Lambton most of the day and I just returned a few minutes ago. I am sure that all will be well, sir."

RICHARD FITZWILLIAM HAD SUFFERED A SERIOUS LEG injury while serving in His Majesty's Army in Spain. A slight pain when walking too quickly was the only evidence that Richard had ever been injured but it prevented him from keeping up with the rapid strides of his cousin. When the men reached the stables, Richard placed his hand on his cousin's shoulder and said, "Darcy, take a deep breath. I am sure Lizzy is safe, maybe she got lost. You said she was with a new footman who could not help her find the way back. Let us get our horses and we will find your wife in short order."

"I am so frightened, I feel just as I did when I got your express telling me Wickham had kidnapped Georgiana. Until I see that my my wife is unharmed..." Darcy bent over and clutched his knees as if in terrible pain, "I love her so much, I cannot live without her."

"Let us away and before you know it we will be sipping tea in the drawing room with your lovely wife."

They mounted their horses and began their search along one of the paths that Darcy knew Elizabeth favored. They had not ridden far when they both spotted a man wearing the Darcy livery lying on the ground. As they got closer, they saw the motionless body in the leaves. They both dismounted and ran toward the footman. "Sanders, Sanders, what happened? Where is Mrs. Darcy? Sanders, where is my wife?" Darcy was shouting by the end of his questioning.

"Let the man come to his senses. Help me sit him up." Sanders had his hand on the back of his head as he slowly began to realize where he was and who was standing before him.

"Sir, I was following Mrs. Darcy when I suppose someone came up behind me and hit me over the head." Sanders continued to massage the back of his head.

"Do you know where Mrs. Darcy is?"

"No sir, I was following her and the next thing I knew, you were trying to wake me. I do not know how long I was knocked out."

"Did she tell you where she was planning to walk today?"

"No sir, I just follow behind the mistress wherever she walks."

"Can find your way back to the house on your own?"

"Yes, sir. I might sit here for a few more minutes and wait for this dizziness to end before I return to the house."

"As you wish, Sanders." Darcy looked at his cousin, "we must find Elizabeth before we lose the sunlight." They mounted their horses and rode further along the path where they had found the footman. After riding for several minutes, Darcy said, "I have an idea. Several weeks ago, I showed Elizabeth our old cave hideout. If she felt she was in danger, she may have gone there to hide."

"I hope you are correct, but I have not been there in nearly twenty years. Lead on, sir." Both men rode in the direction of the tree that had been struck by lightning many years before either of the cousins were born.

As they neared the tree, Richard said he would continue to follow the walking path on horseback. Darcy began shouting his wife's name. He dismounted as he neared the shrubberies shielding the cave's entrance. "Elizabeth! Elizabeth! Can you hear me? Where are you, my love?" Darcy shouted and then stood very still hoping to hear his wife respond. He was soon rewarded for his efforts when he heard the sound of a woman crying. He walked around the shrubs and kneeled down to look into the cave. Darcy had never been so relieved in his life. He saw his beautiful wife sitting against the wall of the cave and rushed to her side, "Elizabeth, are you well? What happened?"

She looked up at her husband and shook her head. "I hardly know, everything happened so quickly. I was walking along the path and I heard some noise behind me. When I turned around, I saw three men standing over the footman's body. Did you find Sanders?" Elizabeth started crying again, "is he dead?"

"No, my love, he has a headache, but he will be well. What happened after you saw the men with Sanders?"

"I was afraid the men would come after me next and I began to run as fast as I was able." She looked down and rubbed her baby bump. "When I saw the old tree, I remembered your hiding spot and I thought it would be a good place to hide *if* I got here before those men saw where I went. I came in here and after running so far, I tried to quiet my breathing, so they could not hear me. I soon heard the voices of the men and the rustling of the leaves as they walked closer. I waited and waited, and I finally heard their voices getting farther away. Even after I thought they were gone, I was too afraid to walk home. I did not know if they were lying in wait for me somewhere. I knew you would find me, but I was so scared."

Darcy knelt before his wife and took her into his arms. "Are you truly well, my love?"

She looked up at her husband with tears in her eyes. "I am well now that you are here, but I was very frightened that those men would find me and try to hurt me and the baby. I kept thinking about Wickham kidnapping Georgiana. What could those men have wanted from me and why did they hurt the footman?"

"Sanders has a bump on his head, but he will be fine. As for who would try to harm you, let us talk about it after I get you home and you have had a nice warm bath."

"You will have to help me up, I have been sitting here for so long, I do not know if my legs can support me." Darcy put his arm around her back, helped his wife stand and slowly led her out of the cave. Once outside, she rose to her full height and shook out her legs, "it feels so good to stand up."

Darcy put his arm around her shoulders, "my love, you are shivering." He removed his coat and placed it around his wife's shoulders. "My horse is on the other side of these shrubs. You can ride with me and we will take a slow walk back to the house. Many members of our staff are walking the woods looking for you and Richard is out here, somewhere. He was with me in my study when we realized that you had not yet returned from your morning walk."

"Richard is here? Were we expecting him?"

"No, but the reason he is here may have something to do with the men who hurt Sanders and who were chasing after you. Let us discuss it after I get you home." Darcy lifted Elizabeth onto his saddle, mounted his horse and sat behind her. He had one arm around his wife's expanded waist and pulled her close as they began their slow return to Pemberley.

She leaned back against her husband, "thank you for finding me. I did not look forward to spending the night in the cave. I knew you would realize where I would hide if I was in danger."

"When Mrs. Reynolds told us you had not yet returned from your morning walk, I confess I was frightened. As soon as I saw the old tree, I prayed you remembered the cave. You are safe now and that is all that matters." Darcy kissed the side of his wife's head as they began their short journey home.

They had only gone a short distance when they heard the sound of a horse coming near them. They both turned to see Richard riding up beside them, "Lizzy, it is very good to see you looking so well."

"Thank you, Richard. I am happy to see you. William told me that your being here may have something to do with Sanders being attacked and those men trying to follow me."

"I told Elizabeth we would discuss it after we return to the house. Richard, she saw three men standing over Sanders' body and they started running after her. Elizabeth hid in our cave and the men did not find her."

Richard was disturbed by what he had just heard and he was grateful that nothing serious befell his cousin's wife. He cleared his throat and said, "let us get back to the house before we lose the sunlight."

She leaned back against her husband and closed her eyes as he tightened his hold on her. They were all relieved that this incident ended so well; the thought of what might have happened was on all of their minds. The threesome slowly made their way back to Pemberley and were soon settled in Darcy's study. Elizabeth resisted her husband's plea that she return to her chambers for a warm bath and some rest. She was sitting on the couch with her feet resting on an ottoman, drinking a cup of tea and enjoying some biscuits.

As Darcy and Richard were sipping their brandy, Elizabeth said, "you two know something that you do not want to tell me. You also know that until I know all of it, I will refuse to go upstairs and enjoy a warm bath."

"Darcy, shall you tell Lizzy, or would you like me to?"

"I am going to sit beside my wife and help keep her warm. You can tell us both everything you know." Darcy brought a blanket to cover Elizabeth's legs and sat on the sofa next to her. He placed his arm around her shoulders and pulled her close into his chest.

Richard was happy to see the love that Darcy and Elizabeth shared and briefly wondered, *I never thought Darcy would make a love match. He never showed interest in any woman during his five Seasons in Town. He resisted the attempts of the many matchmaking mamas' goals to make their daughters Mrs. Darcy. He was even able to withstand my mother's finely-honed matchmaking skills. If Darcy could find happiness and love, can I find someone to love? Will she ever love me the way Lizzy loves Darcy? I never thought about taking a wife while I was a military man but what about now? Can I ever find that one special woman who can love a cantankerous old soldier?*

He redirected his thoughts to the problem at hand. "I started to tell Darcy the problem before we realized you were not home from your walk. The Bow Street Runners, who helped us find and rescue Georgiana in Ramsgate, wrote to me with some discouraging news. If you remember what I told you when I came to Longbourn, when we raided Wickham's house in Ramsgate, we were only able to capture some of Wickham's band of miscreants. The rest of them ran off into the night. It seems that a few of these miserable reprobates are still looking for a big payday by kidnapping someone in the Darcy family to hold for ransom."

Elizabeth's eyes filled with tears as she shook her head in disbelief. "Even from his grave, George Wickham is trying to harm us. It is too much to bear." Through her tears she continued, "we must be sure that Uncle Hugh and Aunt Patricia are informed. They may also be the object of some scheme for money and Georgiana must be very well protected." She paused and then looked at her husband, "all of those men know what Georgiana looks like, William, our dear sister." Darcy used his handkerchief to wipe away his wife's tears. "Georgiana has already gone through so much, we must protect her, but we cannot tell her why we have increased the security. After Ramsgate, it took her so long to trust anyone and overcome her fear of being harmed. We cannot allow her to go through that again. Now, they know what I look like too, but at least, I am aware of the threat."

"Lizzy, of course, you are correct, and you have given me an idea that just might put an end to this danger."

"What is it you are planning? You know that all of Pemberley's resources are at your disposal. We *must* stop these evil men before they can harm anyone else."

"All will be revealed in the fullness of time. First, I must write to my father and make him aware of the potential threat to Georgiana and perhaps, even to my parents. Then we can start to put my plan into action."

Mrs. Reynolds knocked on the door of the study and was quickly asked to enter the room. "Sir, Mr. Laurence has arrived for Mrs. Darcy."

"Thank you, will you check on Sanders and see if he needs anything? If he needs a doctor, Mr. Laurence can see to him after he examines Mrs. Darcy." As he stood and helped Elizabeth to her feet, he turned to his cousin and said, "I pray whatever you are planning will work. For now, I believe it is time for me to escort my wife upstairs. Mr. Laurence will make sure she and the baby are well and then a bath and some rest would do us all some good before we meet for dinner."

As they departed the room, Elizabeth turned and said, "Richard, thank you for coming from Kent to warn us. You are a very welcome guest."

"It is my pleasure to be of service to my favorite cousins. I hope we can end this threat in the next few days. I am happy to be here and I am looking forward to seeing you at dinner."

MRS. REYNOLDS APPROACHED THE DARCYS WHEN THEY came downstairs to dine. "I thought you would like to know that Sanders is in his quarters and said he is feeling well. I offered to have Mr. Laurence see him but he told me that it was not necessary. He assured me he will be perfectly able to return to work after a good night's sleep."

"Thank you for telling us, I am relieved that he was not more seriously injured." The housekeeper smiled at her mistress and walked back toward the kitchen.

"Are you happy now, Mrs. Darcy? Sanders will be fine by tomorrow morning. Let us join Richard, I am certain he is very hungry. He eats as if he were still serving in the army!" She smiled at her husband as they joined their cousin in the drawing room.

CHAPTER 4

Over the course of the next few days, Richard wrote several express letters to his father at Matlock Manor. He wanted to ensure that his parents and Georgiana were as well protected as the occupants of Pemberley. Bethel went out alone to supervise the harvest; with peril hanging over their heads, Darcy refused to let Elizabeth out of his sight. Several days after Richard's arrival, the Darcys walked together in the formal gardens near the house and an armed guard walked closely behind them. "I believe you once told me that your mother designed these beautiful gardens?"

"Yes, after she and father married, she worked for several years with the gardeners and groundskeepers until she was happy with the flower gardens, the arbors and the topiary. She once told me she had plans for a maze but her health began to fail and..."

"I wish she was here so I could thank her for the

beauty all around us." Darcy squeezed her hand on his arm. "I am reminded every day that Pemberley reflects the perfect balance between the natural plants surrounding us and plants within these gardens." Darcy smiled at his wife's comments as they walked in silence enjoying their surroundings. "Do you know what Richard is planning?"

"Not yet. Many letters have been exchanged between him and Uncle Hugh and he assures me that the end of the danger is near."

"I pray you are correct. As much as I love spending time with you, I know how anxious you are to rejoin Mr. Bethel."

Darcy stopped walking and took his wife's hands in his. "Elizabeth, your well-being is my only concern. While you have been resting before dinner, Bethel and I have gone over any problems he has come across during his day working with the tenants."

"I am glad to hear it. Now, shall we return to the house? I told Mrs. Reynolds and Mrs. Covington that I would go over the plans for the Harvest Ball."

"I am delighted that you are helping them. This is the first time in many years that Pemberley will celebrate a Harvest Ball. After my mother passed away, my father refused to host any celebrations here. In the years following his death, Georgiana and I were ill equipped to host any events and last year, we were away on our wedding trip. I pray that this threat is behind us well before we see the Harvest Moon."

As they neared the manor house, they saw Richard walking toward them. "I was just looking for you two. You will be very happily surprised to see who has arrived while you were out." He led them to the doorway of the drawing room where they saw Lord and Lady Matlock drinking tea with Georgiana.

"Georgiana, it is wonderful to have you back home." Elizabeth embraced her sister with unshed tears in her eyes. She was relieved and thankful that no harm had come to this wonderful young girl who had already suffered so much.

"Lizzy, I am so glad to be back. I enjoyed my time with my aunt and uncle, but it is so good to be home." She looked at her sister's midsection and said, "you have gotten so big! When will the baby be here?"

"Not for another two months, I hope you can wait that long?" Everyone smiled at Elizabeth's comment while Darcy greeted his relatives. When the sisters finally separated, Darcy hugged his sister and kissed the top of her head. "Where is Mrs. Annesley?"

"She went to her room to freshen up after our trip. We are both happy to be back home."

Elizabeth embraced Lord and Lady Matlock and thanked them for bringing Georgiana and her companion to Pemberley. "I am very happy to see you both again but after growing up in a houseful of sisters, I keenly felt *this* sister's absence."

"Welcome home, little one. Elizabeth and I have missed you." Darcy looked up and saw his cousin's face and knew that Richard wanted to speak to him privately. "I wonder if you gentlemen would join me in my study for a few minutes? I would like you to look over some plans I have for the spring plantings. Now that the harvest is almost finished, my steward and I have been speaking about which crops to rotate next spring and some other matters I know the ladies would find boring."

Elizabeth was certain the men were going to discuss the threat hanging over the Darcy and Fitzwilliam families. She did not resent being left out of the conversation. She knew that her husband would tell her everything when they were alone later that day.

"Of course, Darcy, I would be happy to look over your plans," Lord Matlock spoke before Richard had a chance to agree.

After the three men entered the study, Darcy spoke first. "What brought you to Pemberley, Uncle? I did not know that Richard had successfully implemented his mysterious plan without my knowledge."

"On the contrary, he did not know we were coming. I will give you the details in a few minutes but let me first tell you that the threat to your family and mine seems to be over."

"Over? How can that be?" Richard asked his father.

"Two days ago, three men were captured near Matlock. They had a bagful of money and some jewelry they had just stolen from the Northam's estate, not far from Matlock Manor. The local magistrate was informed of their location by someone the robbers had met in a local tavern. After several rounds of drinks, one of the thieves began boasting that they were celebrating their new found wealth; they had recently *inherited* some money and jewels. The next morning the man in the tavern called on the magistrate and told him everything he had heard the night before. Finding and capturing three hungover men was easier than they thought, and they are all being held in the local jail.

"I suppose that after their failed attempt to capture Lizzy, they turned their sights from kidnapping to robbery. To be cautious, we brought Georgiana here with several armed guards riding in front of and behind our carriage, as well as two armed men riding on top with the driver. Although the magistrate in Matlock felt that the threat to our family is over, I was not going to take any chances. I suggest you keep your guards on for a few more weeks, by then we can be sure that the danger has passed."

"Thank you for bringing my sister and Mrs. Annesley safely back to us. I would like to think the magistrate is correct, but I will rest easier knowing that armed guards are still protecting us."

"So, I suppose my plan will not see the light of day and I could not be more pleased," said Richard.

"You may tell me all about your plan at another time. Right now, I would like to rejoin the ladies. I wish to look at my wife and sister knowing they are no longer in danger. Uncle, I hope you and Aunt Patricia will join us for dinner and be our guests tonight."

"I believe your aunt has already spoken to Mrs. Reynolds about our usual accommodations." The three men left Darcy's study smiling and rejoined the ladies in the drawing room for refreshments.

LATER THAT AFTERNOON, DARCY AND ELIZABETH WENT to their chambers to change for dinner. Before going downstairs to rejoin their guests, Darcy knocked on the door to his wife's chambers and after he was admitted, he asked Hannah to leave them. "I will ring for you when I am preparing for bed."

"Yes, Mrs. Darcy."

After Hannah was gone, Darcy and Elizabeth sat down on the settee in front of the fireplace. "I know you well enough that I will have no peace until I tell you what my uncle, Richard and I discussed earlier in my study."

"You do know me well, my dear husband," she said as she took her husband's hand in hers.

"It will not take long. In essence, before Richard's plan could be put into place, three criminals were arrested near Matlock after they robbed a nearby estate of money and jewelry while the residents were away traveling. Apparently, the men were watching the Northam's estate and when the observed that there was little or no security, they entered and ransacked the house. The magistrate did not expect there were any other men still on the loose."

"How were they captured so quickly?"

"Evidently, once they got their hands on the money and jewels, they went to the nearest tavern and drank more than enough to loosen their lips. One of the men who overheard their boasting, went to the local magistrate the next day and fortunately, they were easy to track down. It seems that they had so much to drink, they were all still sleeping in their rooms at a nearby inn."

"Are we now safe?" Elizabeth was happy but felt that she would not feel entirely free of the threat until much more time had passed without incident. "Will you tell Georgiana?"

"I do not see any reason to tell her about a threat that no longer exists."

"I agree with you, and now we must go and join our

guests." As they walked toward the staircase, Elizabeth added, "I am trying to be happy about this news but.."

"I know how you are feeling and I will keep the armed guards on for the time being. When we are sure we are completely safe, we can return to our normal security measures."

THE FOLLOWING MORNING, LORD AND LADY MATLOCK returned to Matlock Manor after sharing breakfast with the Darcys and Richard. After their departure, Elizabeth joined the men in Darcy's study while Georgiana and Mrs. Annesley went to the music room. "So, Lizzy, did you sleep well last night knowing the threat is over?"

Elizabeth rubbed her stomach and said, "I have not slept well for some time. This little one tends to practice kicking when I am trying to sleep. But I know what you are talking about and I am happy, but we will not let our guard down until we are quite sure we are out of danger. Richard, we do not believe Georgiana should be told of any of this."

"I agree with you both. I suppose it is now safe for me to get back to Rosings. I thank you for your hospitality."

"Will you not stay for the Harvest Ball? It is less than a week from now; we love having you here and we both appreciate you coming to Pemberley to warn us. Please tell us you will stay and then you can travel back to Kent directly after the Ball."

"How can I say no to such a lovely invitation? I will send a note to Rosings and my steward can handle things for a few more days. I would like to spend more time with Georgiana, I rarely see her now that I am in Kent. I will depart after the party."

"Wonderful, I will let Mrs. Reynolds know you shall remain with us. You know you are one of her favorite people; she always asks Mrs. Covington to serve your favorite foods when you are here," Elizabeth said with a smile.

After speaking with Mrs. Reynolds, Elizabeth encountered Georgiana leaving the music room. "Lizzy, is there anything I can do to help you with the Harvest Ball?"

Although everything was planned, Elizabeth knew her sister wished to be part of the festivities. "Georgie, I do need help organizing the games for the younger children and the gift baskets for the tenants are not yet assembled. I would be very relieved if you could take some of the responsibility off my shoulders. The baby is very active at night and I have not been sleeping well. Shall we meet after my afternoon rest and discuss your ideas?"

"Yes, I will go to my sitting room and write down all

my thoughts. I will speak with you later, and Lizzy, thank you for including me."

"I believe the true meaning of sisterhood is always being available to help your sister in whatever she needs. I thank you for your kind offer. Now, I am off to my chambers for some rest."

"Sleep well, Lizzy."

Meanwhile in his study, Darcy was finally in the frame of mind to ask Richard about his plan to trap the kidnappers. "It hardly seems to matter now; Georgiana is home safely, Elizabeth was unharmed, and my father believes the threat is gone. It seems Lord and Lady Northam being away from their estate and being robbed by Wickham's men eliminated the need for any subterfuge."

"I am certain it was a clever plan, but I am glad it was not needed. I told Elizabeth that we will keep the armed guards on alert for the next few weeks and then return to our usual security if the kidnappers fail to resurface."

"That is a very good plan, cousin. Now tell me who you have invited to the Harvest Ball." The men went over the guest list and were enjoying the relaxing time they were spending together.

CHAPTER 5

Later that afternoon, Georgiana joined Elizabeth in her sitting room and they discussed their plans for the Harvest Ball. Elizabeth was impressed by many of her sister's ideas and she expressed her appreciation. "I think the children will be delighted with the games and activities you have planned for them. The staff will be happy to put together the baskets for the tenants, but I would appreciate you checking on their progress. I know Mrs. Reynolds will also be happy to hear your suggestions. It will not be long before you are presented at Court and make your debut into London's society. Although William and I are in no hurry for you to leave us, you will fall in love with a wonderful man one day and you will be a wonderful mistress of your husband's estate."

"I am grateful for your confidence in me but the thought of my presentation at Court is giving me nightmares. And my coming out Ball is not something I am looking forward to. I wish we could just decide on a certain date that I am out and then I could start attending parties. The idea of being the center of attention for an entire night is not something I am comfortable with. The way I feel now, I can hardly imagine myself as a wife."

"I can understand your feelings but William and I both feel that your debut has been postponed long enough. We will be with you when you have a question or need some encouragement. Aunt Patricia will also be on hand to help us get through all the happy occasions. Now let us join the men for dinner." Elizabeth reached out her hand and the two Darcy sisters walked side by side until they entered the drawing room and greeted Darcy and Richard.

While they were having dinner, they were all excitedly talking about the upcoming Harvest Ball. Elizabeth mentioned to Richard and Georgiana that the new vicar at Kympton had been invited. "Mr. Carter is a young, handsome man who is very well liked by William and me. All his parishioners seem very happy with their new spiritual leader."

"I am sorry I forgot to mention it, but I heard from Mr. Carter. He has regrettably declined our invitation to the Harvest Ball because his sister will be visiting him."

"Do you have any objection to inviting Mr. Carter's sister to attend such an informal event with him? I would hate for his parishioners to miss the opportunity to spend some time with Mr. Carter in a relaxed social setting."

"I think it would be lovely if Mr. Carter and his sister attended our first Harvest Ball in so many years," added Georgiana. "And Richard, I am so glad you will be staying with us until then. It will be so much fun to have you, as well as William, as my dance partners."

"You know I find it very difficult to say no to you. I am very happy to extend my visit until the Harvest Ball; but I must return to Rosings directly after the festivities."

"I suppose this matter is now settled. Richard will remain at Pemberley until the Ball and I will send Mr. Carter a note in the morning. I propose we forego our port tonight. Let us enjoy our time listening to Georgie playing for us, and, perhaps we can even convince my lovely wife to sing."

"I cannot think of anything better!" Richard rose and escorted Elizabeth to the drawing room while Darcy walked his sister to the pianoforte. As she sat down on the bench, Darcy looked at his beautiful sister and said a silent prayer of thanks for her safety. Before he left her seated at the instrument, Darcy leaned over and placed a gentle kiss on her forehead.

"Thank you, brother. It seems like the happiness we

have been missing since our dear parents left us is once again surrounding us."

"I am thankful that we are all safe and happy. However, when you become an aunt, we must be prepared to lose some of the peace and quiet we presently enjoy."

"Yes, I know, but even the sound of a baby crying is a joyful sound. Do you not agree?"

"I could not agree with you more."

Pemberley

September 1813

Dear Mr. Carter,

We are pleased to invite your sister to accompany you to the Harvest Ball on September 23rd. We are looking forward to meeting her and introducing you both to some of the local residents you have not yet had the opportunity to meet. I look forward to your reply.

F. Darcy

Kympton Rectory

September 1813

Dear Mr. Darcy,

I appreciate the kind invitation you have extended to me and my sister, Emily. We will be very happy to attend, and I thank you again for thinking of us.

P. Carter

SHORTLY BEFORE THE HARVEST BALL, JOSIAH HARRIS, the magistrate from Lambton came to see Darcy. As he entered the manor house, his eyes met those of a footman, who immediately turned his head the other way. After he was shown into his study, Darcy asked, "to what do I owe the pleasure of your visit, Mr. Harris?"

"Mr. Darcy, your footman, the man with the very dark hair, I could swear I have seen him before. Has he been in your employ long?"

"No, in fact, I just hired Sanders and another man, a Mr. Johnson, a few weeks ago. I knew I would be busy with Bethel all day and I insisted that Mrs. Darcy be escorted on her daily walks. Do you know him? He came with good references."

"I know I have seen him before; I could never forget his dark hair and eyes. Mr. Darcy, I do not know why, but I think you should keep a close eye on Sanders. If you have any suspicions about his behavior, please send for me at once."

"He was injured by the would-be kidnappers while

he was escorting Mrs. Darcy. Do you think his head wound was a ruse?"

"If he is up to no good, he could have easily pretended to be hit on the head. Was he examined by a doctor?" Darcy shook his head in response. "I will try to figure out where I have seen him and if I think there is any threat to your family, I will notify you immediately. If I need to see his references, I assume you still have them."

"I trust your judgement and your education, even though you were an Oxford man." Darcy grinned at the magistrate, "I will look for his letters of recommendation later today and have them delivered to your office. Thank you for the warning, Mr. Harris but there must have been another reason for your coming here."

"I came to give you some good news. I received a note from Mr. Irwin, the magistrate in Matlock. He told me the three men he apprehended in connection to the robbery at Lord and Lady Northam's estate, confessed. They said they originally came to Derbyshire in order to kidnap a member of your family and hold them for a very large ransom. They admitted their guilt in an effort to have their sentences reduced from hanging to transportation."

"At least, there is that good news. We will all sleep a little easier knowing we are no longer threatened by those men. I thank you for coming here yourself to deliver the good news. May I offer you some brandy?"

"I thank you, but I must be getting back to town. I noticed a few of the extra armed guards you have stationed around the house. I no longer believe their services are needed. I know you maintain an excellent security force at all times. Mr. Darcy, keep your eyes on your new footman. Good day, sir."

"Thank you for taking the time to deliver the good news in person. I will do as you ask regarding Sanders."

Darcy did not wish to worry his wife or sister, so he said nothing about Mr. Harris's warning about the newly hired footman. He planned to speak to Richard about the magistrate's concerns at the first opportunity. He would also speak to Mrs. Reynolds and ask her to make certain she did not ask that Sanders escort Elizabeth or Georgiana. Mrs. Reynolds knew Darcy well enough not to question his request.

DARCY ENTERED HIS WIFE'S CHAMBERS AFTER THEY HAD prepared for bed. "Why are you walking with your hands behind you? I know you are hiding something." She was trying to peek behind her husband's back, but he teased her and kept turning away from her until she stayed in one place.

Darcy approached his wife and bent to kiss her head.

"Do you know what today is, Mrs. Darcy?"

"Today?" She paused and tried to think. "Oh, my goodness, today is September the seventeenth, our first wedding anniversary. With all the worries about the kidnappers and planning for the Harvest Ball, I suppose I completely lost track of the date. Happy anniversary to you, my dearest husband."

"Happy anniversary to you, my beloved wife. And now, here is the part where you get to see what I am holding."

"William, I am so sorry I have no gift for you. I feel terrible about forgetting the day we were joined in marriage; the happiest day of my life."

Darcy showed Elizabeth the small box he had been holding behind his back. When he handed it to her he said, "You need not think of this as an anniversary gift; it is just something I thought you would like to have."

"Well, you have certainly piqued my interest." Elizabeth removed the ribbon and opened the box to find a beautiful gold locket nestled in the silk lining. "It is so beautiful. Thank you, William, I will treasure it always."

"It has today's date engraved on the back and if you open it, you will see there are spaces for several pictures. I thought that when the baby is old enough, we can have a portrait done and a miniature can be placed in your locket. And if we are so blessed, there is room for several more miniatures."

"What a wonderful idea from my wonderful husband. I will cherish it and I look forward to adding our child's portrait and, I pray, several more." Elizabeth handed the locket to her husband and lifted her hair so he could close the clasp. "I still feel terrible that I have nothing for you."

"Elizabeth, you should know by now, that having you in my life; every day, every night, as my wife, my friend, my partner and the mother of my child is all that I will ever need. Your love for me is the only gift I will ever want."

Elizabeth reached up and caressed her husband's face. "You shall always have the gift of my love." She took his hand and led him to the bed where they spent the remainder of the night, celebrating their anniversary by expressing their love for each other.

THE FOLLOWING DAY, DARCY ASKED HIS COUSIN TO JOIN him in his study after breakfast. When the two men were seated, Darcy rose from his desk chair and opened the study door and looked into the hallway. He closed the door firmly and looked at Richard, "perhaps we should speak outside."

"My my, you are being quite mysterious!"

"Just cautious cousin, just cautious."

When they were far from the house, Darcy began, "Richard, I need your help. Mr. Harris, the magistrate in Lambton was here yesterday. As he walked toward my study, he thought he recognized one of our new footmen. He said he knew he had seen him before but could not remember where. Mr. Harris warned us to keep an eye on Sanders and let him know immediately if we see anything suspicious. I did not tell Mrs. Reynolds why, but I asked her not to ask Sanders to escort Elizabeth or Georgiana when they leave the house."

"You think that Sanders was involved in the kidnapping scheme all along? Why are you keeping him on? Why is he not already with his friends in gaol?"

"He has a right to work and came with good references. Until we know otherwise, we should just keep our eyes on him without letting him know that we suspect him."

"Darcy, you have given me an idea. What would you say to setting a trap for Sanders? If he is innocent, we will soon know it. If he is guilty, he should be in irons as quickly as possible."

"You were an accomplished military strategist, I will do whatever you think is best."

THE HARVEST BALL WAS SCHEDULED FOR SEPTEMBER twenty-third, the day that Elizabeth had been assured by the groundskeepers would also bring the Harvest Moon. They explained to her that because the moon rises so soon after sunset, the brightness of the Harvest Moon enables the farmers to continue to harvest their crops until well after sundown. The Harvest Moon can last for several days which is another reason it is celebrated by the farmers. Elizabeth had learned from Mrs. Reynolds, that according to tradition, the party was also a celebration of the food grown on the land and a successful harvest at the end of the farming year. Elizabeth and Georgiana liked the idea of having the musicians play many of the local folk songs. The festivities would also include games for the children and food and dancing for everyone.

Mrs. Reynolds, Cook and the entire kitchen staff had prepared an impressive feast for their guests; friends, members of the local gentry and the tenants alike. Elizabeth hoped it would be a high-spirited occasion, one that would mingle the partygoers' expression of gratitude with jovial good cheer. Georgiana had helped fill and decorate the baskets of fruit and food which all the tenants would be given at the end of the festivities. Elizabeth and Mrs. Reynolds found an idea they liked among the notes describing many of the previous Harvest celebrations. They decorated the room with various symbols of the harvest: corn stalks, bales of hay and baskets overflowing with pumpkins, gourds and other seasonal food.

CHAPTER 6

THE HARVEST BALL 1813

The night of the Harvest Ball arrived at last. Darcy and Elizabeth stood near the front door and happily received all their guests. Elizabeth had come to know most of the tenants in the past year and she was very happy to welcome them all to Pemberley. When Mr. Carter arrived, he was accompanied by his sister whom he introduced as Lady Emily Howard. Lady Emily was a very attractive young woman who was dressed in a simple lavender gown. When the Darcys greeted her, she explained that she hesitated before accepting their invitation because she was in mourning for her husband. She had not planned to join them, but her brother encouraged her to attend even if she could not dance. "We are very happy you are here with us, and you have our sincere condolences." Peter left his sister talking with the Darcys and walked toward the ballroom to greet his parishioners.

"Thank you, Mrs. Darcy. My brother told me I would like you as soon as we met."

Elizabeth smiled at the compliment and asked, "Will you stay in Derbyshire long, Lady Howard?"

"Mrs. Darcy, please call me Emily, or Lady Emily if you must. I have never felt comfortable with being called Lady Howard. I believe I will remain in Derbyshire for the foreseeable future. Upon my late husband's death, his younger brother quickly moved his family into the Howard estate in Surrey. I am hoping to remain on good terms with the family, so I quickly moved my things out of there as well as Howard House in London."

"In that case, we welcome you to Pemberley and hope we will see much more of you while you are in Derbyshire." Lady Emily was still speaking with Elizabeth when Richard came out of the ballroom and walked toward them. He did not recognize the beautiful petite blond woman Elizabeth was speaking to. "Richard, I would like you to meet one of our guests. Lady Howard, allow me to introduce you to our cousin, Richard Fitzwilliam; Richard, may I present Lady Howard. Lady Howard is the sister of Mr. Carter, the new vicar at Kympton."

"It is a pleasure to meet you, Lady Howard. May I escort you to the ballroom?" Lady Emily thought the tall, dark-haired man she had just met was very attractive. *He has the most beautiful blue eyes. He certainly looks like he has done a great deal of physical labor; he fills out his dinner jacket quite well. Stop it Emily! Try to remember you are in mourning.*

"Yes, but only if you call me Emily or Lady Emily." He smiled and nodded his agreement with her request before offering her his arm. As they walked together toward the ballroom, Richard silently cursed the painful souvenir of the war which he carried with him. Although his leg might suffer from the activity, he gathered his courage and asked, "May I have the honor of dancing the second set with you, Lady Emily?" She was a very beautiful woman, but Richard wondered if she was kind enough to dance with a man with an occasional limp.

"Mr. Fitzwilliam, I regret that I must decline; I am still in mourning for my husband."

"You have my sincere condolences for your loss, madam." Although they would not be sharing a dance, Richard was immediately taken by this lovely young woman and her penetrating green eyes. After he escorted her to the ballroom, he sat beside her at one of the many tables set up around the dance floor.

After speaking about the décor and number of people in attendance, Richard was baffled by what he should say next so he asked, "Lady Emily, may I bring you some lemonade?"

"Thank you, I would enjoy having some." When he returned with their beverages, he sat beside Lady Emily and they spent the first set chatting. He told her about his close relationship with the Darcys and that he was the co-guardian of Georgiana. She told him a little about growing up in Suffolk with her two older brothers but never said a word about her late husband.

ELIZABETH WAS ANXIOUSLY AWAITING THE BINGLEYS' arrival; she had not seen her dear sister in many weeks. Jane was kept very busy with her daughter, Maddie, and she was quite busy planning the Harvest Ball. Elizabeth did not venture from the confines of Pemberley due to an overabundance of caution on her husband's part. He did not want his wife to be jostled around the inside of a carriage unless it was absolutely necessary.

Finally, the Bingleys' coach pulled up to the house and the Darcys stepped outside to greet them. They were quite surprised when, after Charles helped Jane from the carriage, he turned back to help his sister, Caroline. As Jane embraced Elizabeth, she whispered in her ear, "Lizzy, I am so sorry, we did not know Caroline was coming to visit us. We were shocked when she showed up at our door this morning and we could hardly leave her home. She is so well acquainted with you all and we did not wish to miss your party. I hope you and William do not mind too much."

Caroline Bingley was well known to the Darcys from the time the Bingleys resided in Hertfordshire. She had also visited Birchwood Manor while Elizabeth was residing there. Caroline was an attractive woman when she was not wearing a sneer or looking down her nose at the people around her. She was tall and thin and had the same reddish-blonde hair as her brother. Her sister, Luisa Hurst, married for several years and living in London, was dark haired and shorter in stature than her siblings. Elizabeth did not answer her sister but turned away from Jane and walked to where Caroline Bingley was nearing the front steps. Elizabeth smiled and said, "Miss Bingley, welcome to Pemberley. We are delighted you could join us."

Elizabeth's kindness surprised Caroline and she simply curtsied and said, "I thank you for the welcome, Mrs. Darcy," she smiled as she entered Pemberley. *I should have been the mistress of this grand estate and the likes of that country chit, Eliza Bennet, would never be permitted through the door. Well, maybe the kitchen door, she could always work here as a maid. All the time I wasted chasing after Mr. Darcy and in the end, he married a woman with no accomplishments, no sense of fashion, no social skills and no connections to London's high society. The next thing you know, she will allow horses to graze in the music room!*

Darcy and Elizabeth remained in the entry hall to greet their late arriving guests. When they entered the ballroom, he smiled at his beautiful wife when he saw that every aspect of her meticulous planning had come to fruition. All their guests were busy chatting, drinking punch and lemonade and partaking of all the delicious food Mrs. Covington and the kitchen staff had worked so hard to produce. The musicians were beginning to tune their instruments when Darcy and Elizabeth walked to the center of the dance floor. "Ladies and gentlemen, may I have your attention for a moment." When the people gathered in the ballroom noticed their hosts attempting to gain their attention, they all quieted to listen to the master of Pemberley. Just as Darcy began to speak, a ball rolled across the floor in front of him, followed by two laughing boys. Darcy picked up the ball and handed it to one of the children. The boys knew who stood before them and tried to bow as best they could. Everyone laughed at the boys' lack of inhibition and their feeble attempt to show respect to the master of the estate.

"As I was saying, Mrs. Darcy and I are very happy to welcome you all to the Harvest Ball. Most of you know that we have not held this happy event at Pemberley for many, many years. Now is the time for us all to look ahead." Darcy looked down at his wife and her very large front and smiled. "We thank you all for your hard work which has resulted in a very successful harvest and we look forward to welcoming you all to next year's Harvest Ball." All the guests began to clap and cheer for the return of this happy event and the joy and optimism which now pervaded Pemberley. When the cheering died down, Darcy continued, "before we begin the dancing, I would like to ask Mr. Carter to lead us in a prayer of thanks."

Mr. Carter walked toward the Darcys and said, "friends, let us bow our heads. This harvest celebration reminds us of all the good things God gives us. This gratitude to the Almighty moves us to share with others who are not so fortunate. Many dishes have been prepared tonight which will be distributed to those members of our congregation who are most in need. We thank all of you for your labors in the past growing season and we thank God for a most successful harvest. Let us all say, amen."

Looking around the ballroom, Caroline could hardly believe her eyes; the room was decorated with straw men and pumpkins! Pumpkins! She was appalled by the lack of fashion and proper decorum that she was accustomed to in London. *I cannot believe that Pemberley, one of the grandest estates in all of England, has sunk to this undignified level; no doubt the work of that country bumpkin who is now mistress. If I had married Darcy, none of this riffraff would ever be allowed to enter through the front door. Although I was quite impressed by the words and confidence of the handsome young vicar. Still, the total lack of fashion, decorum and manners is truly shocking!*

While in London, Caroline attended services almost every Sunday, but she had never been interested in what the man in the front of the church had to say. She was always too busy looking around to see if there were any eligible men or members of the nobility attending the service. Several minutes later, she was standing with Jane and Charles still musing about how low the Darcy family had fallen when Mr. Carter walked by. "Pray excuse me for the intrusion but are you not Mrs. Darcy's sister and brother? We met once before, I am Peter Carter, the vicar at Kympton."

"How lovely to see you again, Mr. Carter. We appreciated your prayer. Allow me to introduce my sister, Miss Caroline Bingley," Jane said. "Caroline, may I present Peter Carter, the vicar at Kympton." Peter Carter bowed, and Caroline curtsied while trying to take a measure of the attractive, tall man before her.

"Miss Bingley, it is a pleasure to meet you."

"Thank you, sir, I am happy to meet you, as well."

They could hear the musicians warming up when Peter Carter said, "I realize that we have just been introduced but may I ask if you are available for the first set?"

"Mr. Carter, I would be delighted." Caroline could not refuse his offer and she placed her hand on Mr. Carter's arm as the couples were lining up for the dance. As Caroline and Mr. Carter walked away, Jane and Charles smiled at each other, each silently praying that perhaps Caroline had finally met someone to marry and start her own life. Jane thought, *as much as we would like her to meet someone, we must be honest about our sister. It is highly unlikely that Caroline would consider anyone without a large fortune and a title.*

As they were dancing, Caroline admired his fine clothes and his calm demeanor, but she knew that a vicar must live simply. She had never heard his name while attending London society events, so she knew he must be a person of no significance in the *ton*. Although he could never be considered as a candidate to become her husband, she decided that dancing with a tall, handsome and well-dressed man was better than standing with her brother and Jane watching everyone else having a good time.

After their dance, Peter escorted Caroline to the refreshments table. Although she did not know why, she was intrigued by the vicar. He was very good looking and seemed to be very happy with his lot in life. He was also an excellent dancer and easy to converse with. While they sipped their lemonade, she asked, "if you do not mind me asking, how did you come to the Church?"

"I do not mind at all. My older brother has been groomed his entire life to take over my family's business interests. I never had a taste for financial matters, but I have always felt a calling to serve God. I attended Cambridge and shortly after finishing there, I took orders. As part of my training to be a vicar, I first worked as a curate in a parish near my family's estate in Suffolk. When I heard that the living in Kympton was available, I came to Derbyshire and met with Mr. Darcy and Mr. Hatcher, the retiring vicar.

"Several weeks later, I received a letter from Mr. Darcy offering me the living at Kympton. I moved into the parsonage in August and my sister, Emily, I should say, Lady Howard, came to stay with me earlier this month. As I am not married, she has been acting as my hostess and has been very helpful. She has chosen some lovely pieces of furniture to replace some of the worn out items and has helped me hire a small staff."

So, his parents have their own estate in Suffolk, and I have to meet the second son. When will I meet the oldest son of a wealthy family?

"Your sister is Lady Howard?"

"Yes, she is now a widow, Lord Howard died several months ago, and Emily is still in mourning. She came to Derbyshire to have some peace and quiet after living in London. She accompanied me here tonight."

"I am sorry to hear of her loss, my condolences."

"Thank you for your kind words.

Certainly, no one has ever thanked me for being kind before. I remember meeting Lord Howard once or twice at parties in London. He had quite a reputation as a gambler, heavy drinker and a womanizer. I wonder what drew him and Lady Howard together?

Peter escorted her back to her family and before he left her he bowed and said, "It was a pleasure meeting you Miss Bingley and I enjoyed our dance and conversation."

Caroline curtsied and said, "Yes, it was very pleasant." As she looked around the room, she glanced at the Darcys standing at the side of the dance floor and watched them while they were quietly speaking to one another. *I will never know what arts and allurements Eliza Bennet used to trap Mr. Darcy into marriage. They do appear to be happy together and will obviously be welcoming a child very soon. Darcy was always drawn to that hoyden, even in Hertfordshire, he could not take his eyes off her. Heaven knows why!*

While Richard was dancing with Georgiana, his eyes kept returning to where Lady Emily was sitting on the outskirts of the ballroom. She was rarely alone; at various times she was joined by Elizabeth, Peter Carter and many of her brother's parishioners stopped at her table to welcome her. *I suppose I am not the only one who found Lady Emily engaging and pleasant to speak with.*

When Elizabeth sat with Lady Emily, they discussed some of the many changes they both experienced when they moved to Derbyshire from warmer portions of England. "I hope you were not upset when Mr. Fitzwilliam asked to escort you to the ballroom so shortly after you were introduced. He is a very dear member of our family and we do not see him as often as we once did since he moved to Kent. We are so happy he was able to join us tonight."

"I was very happy to meet him. When he asked me to dance, I was sorry to disappoint him. He appeared to understand that my refusal came from my adherence to the customs of our society."

"Yes, I am sure you are correct. Richard is one of the finest men I have ever met." The two women smiled at each other. "Lady Emily, I hope to speak with you again this evening, but I must greet some of our other guests and speak to my husband." Both women rose and curtsied and Elizabeth turned to greet some of the tenants.

THE MUSICIANS WERE WARMING UP FOR ANOTHER SET when Elizabeth glanced up at her husband with a pleading look in her eyes. "We spoke about this. No dancing for you tonight, my love. I do not wish our babe to be born in the ballroom."

"I know I agreed to stay off my feet as much as possible, but you know how I love to dance."

"Next year, I promise you I will dance you off your feet while our beautiful child sleeps upstairs in the nursery."

"I am looking forward to that, sir."

Darcy raised his wife's hand to his lips and said

quietly, "I hope you know that I love you very much, Mrs. Darcy."

"Your secret is safe with me, Mr. Darcy."

Later in the party, Richard was walking toward the terrace for some fresh air when he heard a child crying. When he turned around, he saw that Lady Emily was kneeling down in front of the little boy and was attempting to comfort the child. She was evidently successful; the young boy was smiling when he raised his arms to be held and was quickly in her embrace. A moment later, the boy's mother came to claim her child and thanked Lady Emily for caring for her son. While watching the interaction between Lady Emily and the child, Richard felt a stirring in his heart which he had never felt before. At that moment, he knew he would be spending a lot of time thinking about the beautiful but guarded Lady Emily.

At the end of the evening, Richard approached the object of his attraction, and she smiled when she said, "I am very happy to have met you, Mr. Fitzwilliam. I trust that we will see you in a few days at Michaelmas services."

"Alas, I regret that we will not meet again any time soon, for I return to Kent in a few days. I have been invited to return to Pemberley for the festive season, but for now I must depart; I am afraid that I have neglected my duties long enough. The Darcys are very good hosts and I have enjoyed my time here at

Pemberley, especially meeting you tonight." Richard took Emily's hand and bowed over it before he turned to walk away. What Richard could not see were Lady Emily's eyes following him until she lost sight of him as he entered the ballroom.

CHAPTER 7

Richard and Darcy waited until the day after the party to put their plan to trap the footman into action. The day before, Darcy had received a note from Mr. Harris stating that he remembered that he had seen Sanders riding through Lambton with three other dirty, shabbily dressed men. Harris also informed Darcy that none of Sanders' references were authentic and he would arrive with some of his men early in the morning after the party.

Darcy and Richard met Harris by the stables just after dawn and the magistrate explained how the criminals planned their attempted kidnapping. "Their movements through our area were not difficult to track; four very dirty, unkempt men were easily spotted wherever they went. After I saw them ride through Lambton, they ended up in Bakewell. That is where they got Sanders cleaned up and into some decent clothes. From Bakewell, they left Sanders on the outskirts of Lambton and that is when he applied for the job here. The others waited nearby for his signal before they attempted to kidnap Mrs. Darcy."

"I would like to strangle them all for trying to hurt my wife."

"His cohorts have already faced justice and Sanders will soon follow." Darcy, Richard and Harris discussed exactly how they planned to catch Sanders in the act of trying to kidnap Elizabeth. Roberts, one of the younger stable boys was dressed in Elizabeth's clothes and a large pillow was tied around his waist to make him look as much like his mistress as possible. To further disguise him, Roberts wore Elizabeth's long pelisse and bonnet.The boy was given precise instructions regarding what to say and do when the time came. After breakfast, Darcy asked Georgiana and Elizabeth to wait upstairs until he or Richard came for them. "Nothing is wrong but please follow my request." Mrs. Reynolds had been asked to keep Sanders occupied in the kitchen until Darcy asked to see the footman. After the women were escorted to Elizabeth's sitting room, he asked for Sanders to meet him near the front door. "Mrs. Darcy wishes to take a walk today, in fact, I believe she is already awaiting you near the stables. I would escort her myself, but Bethel is in my study with some urgent business. Go quickly, Sanders, she should not walk on her own." The footman bowed and was soon out of the house.

As soon as Sanders was walking toward the stables, Darcy and Richard followed him while hiding behind the trees along the path so they could not be seen. Roberts was standing near a tree with his back to Sanders. As soon as the stable boy began walking, the footman quickly followed and as he neared the young man, he began to quicken his pace. Before Harris or any of his men could do anything, Sanders came up behind his prey and held a knife to the neck of the stable boy. "Do not think about screaming Mrs. Darcy. As long as your husband pays me the money I ask for, you will be safe." As he was instructed to do, Roberts pretended to faint and was face down on the leaves before Sanders could prevent Elizabeth's impostor from falling. As he bent down to see to his victim, Mr. Harris and his men walked toward him with their pistols drawn and pointed at the would-be kidnapper.

"Stand back, Sanders and keep your hands up. If you make one false move, I will be more than happy to shoot you myself."

"Do not shoot! I have done nothing wrong!" As soon as Harris was close enough to see Sanders clearly, he was certain he was the man he saw riding through Lambton with the three other criminals who had been arrested in Matlock.

"You did nothing but attempt to kidnap Mrs. Darcy!" One of his men kneeled next to the body in the leaves and helped Roberts rise and turn toward Sanders.

Sanders was shocked to see a young man standing before him. "Who is this? You trapped me! You have no proof I did anything wrong!"

"If you do not think telling me not to scream while holding a knife to my neck is nothing!" Roberts looked at Harris, who had been joined by Darcy and Richard. "He said, 'as long as your husband pays me the money I ask for, you will be safe'."

Mr. Harris added, "we all heard everything you said to young Roberts. There will be no shortage of witnesses to make sure you hang for what you tried to do."

Darcy walked toward the man who might have killed his wife and unborn child. He grabbed Sanders by his neckcloth and seethed, "I trusted you. I gave you a job and this is how you repaid me. You tried to destroy my life for money. Your friends are all being transported, but it is up to the magistrate to determine *your* fate." Darcy turned away from the man who could have harmed the person he loved most in the world. "Mr. Harris, I thank you for warning us about Sanders. Would you please remove his disgusting carcass from my land?"

"With pleasure, Mr. Darcy." Sanders hands had been tied behind his back and Mr. Harris pushed him toward the wagon they had brought to Pemberley that morning.

As the cousins walked near the house, they paused

and looked at each other. "Richard, I cannot thank you enough. Your plan worked beautifully, and no one was hurt. If he had succeeded," Darcy tried to remain composed while thinking of how the entire scheme could have ended differently. After a moment he said, "he did not succeed and now I will rest easy knowing my family is truly safe." Richard patted his cousin on the back and smiled as they entered the house.

"Would you like me to be with you when you tell Lizzy and Georgiana?"

"Yes, if you do not mind." The cousins climbed the stairs and entered the sitting room. They found the women reading quietly but they both rose to their feet when the men entered.

"What happened? Why did we have to remain in my sitting room? Are you both well?" Elizabeth asked one question quickly after another.

Richard walked to Georgiana and kissed her head while Darcy kissed Elizabeth's hand and escorted her back to a chair. "Richard, I will let you tell them what happened."

Richard stood before them and told them what had transpired since Mr. Harris recognized Sanders the day he came to Pemberley. Both women had tears in their eyes as they listened, not believing how terrible things could have been.

"Wickham, again!" Georgiana said angrily. "I was such a fool to believe anything that man ever said to me! I was blindfolded shortly after Mrs. Younge brought me to Wickham's house. I wish I had seen their faces and could have recognized Sanders weeks ago." Georgiana was relieved they were all safe, but she was still angry with herself; she had been Wickham's first victim and if the footman and his cohorts had their way, Elizabeth would have suffered greatly at the hands of the nefarious gang.

"Georgiana, you must not blame yourself," Elizabeth said quietly. "We were preyed upon by men who would not be satisfied until they collected the money Wickham promised them. As you said, we are safe and now I can think about preparing the nursery for this little one," Elizabeth said as she rubbed her very large baby bump.

"I can only speak for myself but is anyone else hungry?" Richard asked as a way to change the topic of conversation. "Planning and capturing a criminal has given me an appetite!" They all laughed with relief that this terrible threat was behind them.

"Richard, I cannot recall a time in our lives when you did not have an appetite!" Darcy teased as everyone rose to go downstairs and enjoy a meal, knowing they were all safe.

As they were preparing for dinner, her husband

entered her chambers just as Hannah was leaving. She slowly rose and walked to her husband who embraced her tightly. "William, was Roberts hurt in any way? He should be compensated for the risk he took in order to save me from harm," she said with tears in her eyes.

"Roberts has been promoted to senior stable hand and will be compensated accordingly. I tried to give him a reward, but he refused to take it. He told me he was happy to help you and that while you were still riding, you were always very kind to him."

"Thank you. Roberts risked his life for me and after the baby is born, I will speak to him and thank him myself. Let us go down and join the others. We have much to celebrate tonight."

Darcy kissed her quickly. "Yes, Mrs. Darcy, tonight, I am a very grateful man."

AT BREAKFAST THE NEXT MORNING, RICHARD announced that it was time he returned to Rosings. Before he left, he asked Darcy if they could speak privately before his departure. As soon as they entered the study, he asked, "what do you know about Lady Emily? She told me at the Ball that she could not dance because she is mourning her husband. Did you ever meet the late Lord Howard?"

"No, I do not believe I ever met him. All I know is what I have heard from Mr. Carter and some rumors floating around London. I know that Lady Howard's family, the Carters, are very successful and hard-working and their large fortune was made in trade, farm exports, I believe. I heard that her parents strongly encouraged Emily, their only daughter, to marry well, meaning a man with a title. Less than a year after their wedding, her husband was returning home after a long night of drinking, gambling and womanizing when he was set upon by footpads.

"Carter told me that shortly after Lord Howard's death, the younger brother, the new Lord Howard, quickly moved into the family's London townhouse as well as their country estate with his wife and young daughter. They did not exactly throw Lady Emily out, but she was made to feel unwelcome and she came to Derbyshire to be with her brother. After her husband's death, she felt quite lonely and wanted to be with her family. She came to Kympton to be with her brother because I believe she was still very angry with her parents. It will take some time before she can forgive them for forcing her to marry a man she did not love. It appears they were far less interested in their daughter's feelings and only cared about how her marriage to Lord Howard would elevate the Carter family's standing in the *ton*."

"Well, now I understand why she seems very closed off. She is a beautiful young woman who has been hurt by many people."

"I take it that you would like to spend more time

with Lady Emily; perhaps she will still be in Kympton during the Christmas holidays. I know Elizabeth is planning to invite Mr. Carter to our Christmas dinner and the Yuletide party for our tenants. If she remains with her brother, we will be sure to invite her to all our celebrations."

"Thank you, I appreciate the information. Whether or not it will help my desire to know her better, I feel I have finally met a woman I could imagine as my wife."

"I hope you get what you want. She would be a very lucky woman to have you as a husband."

"I want a woman who looks at me the way Lizzy looks at you. I do not think I could settle for less. You married for love and I plan to do the same. Is Lady Emily the woman for me? Only time will tell."

Darcy rose and shook his cousin's hand. "Richard, thank you for coming and letting us know about the terrible threat we faced. We have kept you here long enough and I understand that you must return to Rosings. We are looking forward to having you join us in December when our family will have a new member. We plan to have the baby's christening while everyone is here for the holidays. I am hopeful Elizabeth will be recovered from the birth by then. I worry that she is taking too much on, but she assures me that we have an extremely competent staff to help."

"Lizzy will be fine; sometimes you worry like an old hen. Farewell, Darcy! I look forward to receiving an announcement of my new cousin's birth." The men embraced, and Richard walked out the door.

Darcy sat down at his desk and went over the conversation he just had with his cousin. *Richard is falling in love with Lady Emily. She seems like a pleasant woman, but I think Richard is getting ahead of himself. If I tell Elizabeth, I know she will do everything she can to play the matchmaker. As Richard said, only time will tell.* He realized he had been staring off into space long enough and picked up a stack of papers he needed to read.

LATER THAT DAY, ELIZABETH WAS HOLDING HER husband's arm as they walked near Pemberley's lake. "Do you remember what I told you about my dreams while I was waiting for you to return to Hertfordshire?"

"I remember that you told me you dreamt about this lake although you had never been here."

"Night after night, I dreamt of us holding the hands of a little boy as we walked along the lake. You were holding a little girl in your arms and we were all laughing."

"In a few weeks, at least a part of your dream will come true. Someday, I pray we will be blessed with another child. All will be well, Elizabeth, and you know I will do anything I can to make all your dreams come true." Elizabeth leaned into Darcy's arm and he kissed the top of her head as they slowly walked back to the manor house.

~

WHEN RICHARD RETURNED TO ROSINGS, HIS DAYS WERE busy from dawn to dusk working on his estate. He was relieved to see how well his steward, Mr. Miller, had done in his absence and together they helped the tenants finish the harvest. Richard was faced with all the responsibilities he had neglected while he was in Derbyshire and he got to work. He had little time to think of anything else other than the tasks required of the master of an estate the size of Rosings. However, many nights, despite his physical fatigue, he lay awake in bed, unable to fall asleep. He repeatedly saw Lady Emily's face and remembered how she cared for a stranger's child at the Harvest Ball. Only when he pictured her face and heard her voice in his head, was he able to sleep. In the morning, he often awakened remembering that he had dreamt of this beautiful, intriguing woman.

NOW THAT THE HARVEST BALL WAS BEHIND THEM, THE residents of Pemberley anxiously prepared to welcome a new member to the family. Every day, Elizabeth and Mrs. Reynolds worked together preparing the nursery. Over and over, her mistress asked the housekeeper the same questions regarding the necessary furniture, bedding, and clothing that the newest Darcy would require. The housekeeper knew that her mistress was not being difficult; she was exhibiting the normal behaviors of an expectant mother preparing for the birth of her first child. Georgiana and Mrs. Annesley kept busy creating some beautifully embroidered garments for the baby.

Darcy found it difficult to sit at his desk and focus on the work before him. He endlessly paced back in forth in front of the fireplace in his study trying to work off some of his anxiety and fear. Childbirth had taken the life of his beloved mother and Darcy repeatedly reminded himself that his lovely wife had always been much healthier than Lady Ann Darcy. He prayed daily that his wife would not succumb as his mother had.

One evening as October came to a close, everyone was seated in the drawing room after dinner. Elizabeth was busily occupied with embroidering a blanket for the baby when she felt she was being stared at. She looked up to see her husband, sister and Mrs. Annesley all watching her intently. Elizabeth blew out a long sigh before she said, "I thank you all for your concern, but you must believe me; I will let you know when the baby decides it is time to be born. Watching my every movement will not make the baby come any faster."

"Lizzy, it is just that we are all so excited and happy about the baby. Are you certain we cannot get you anything?"

"I thank you, Georgie, but I am very comfortable sitting here with my feet up." She thought she would give her sister something to do. "Perhaps, a cup of tea would be nice."

At her request, three people rushed to their feet and approached the cart which held the after-dinner tea service. At the sight of everyone moving at once, Elizabeth began to laugh, and she was quickly joined by all three people eager to be the person to pour her a cup of tea.

Elizabeth was under the assumption that Mr. Laurence and a midwife would help deliver the baby when the time came. Jane happily agreed to come to Pemberley to be with her sister and help keep her calm. What she did not know is that her husband had arranged for the top accoucheur in London, Sir William Knighton, to be on hand to assist her with the birth.

CHAPTER 8

Several days later, Darcy awoke in the early morning hours to find that he was alone in bed. He quickly sat up and saw that his wife was sitting in a nearby armchair with her eyes closed, slowly rubbing her belly. Darcy quietly rose and donned his robe before approaching and kneeling beside Elizabeth. "Are you well, my love?" He asked quietly.

"I am well, but I believe our child has decided it is time to join us."

"Have no worries, I will call for Mrs. Reynolds and Hannah and I will have one of the footmen retrieve Sir Knighton and Mr. Laurence from Lambton and Jane from Birchwood."

"Who is Sir Knighton? I thought Mr. Laurence, Jane and the midwife would care for me."

"Sir William Knighton is the foremost accoucheur in London and I asked him to come to Derbyshire to be with you when it is time for the babe to be born. I think that having Sir Knighton, Mr. Laurence, Jane and the midwife will ensure you have the best of care."

Elizabeth was suddenly gripped by a strong labor pain and it took her a moment before she said, "William, do whatever you feel is necessary but please, do it quickly!"

Darcy rang for his wife's maid but lost his patience and opened the door to the hallway and began shouting for Mrs. Reynolds and Hannah. They quickly responded to his summons and they were each given instructions as to what was required to be done. The two women soon returned to Mrs. Darcy's chambers and prepared her for the imminent birth of the newest member of the Darcy family. When they were finished with their tasks, Darcy was readmitted to his wife's chambers. Mrs. Reynolds told him that he could not remain with his wife, "I will be happy to come and get you when it is time to rejoin Mrs. Darcy. Everyone she needs to care for her will arrive shortly. I assure you that I will make certain that she is getting the best care possible. Now, out you go!" She had known him since he was a small boy and it was not often she needed to speak to him as if he were still a child.

He walked to the side of his wife's bed and took her

hand in his as he quietly said, "Elizabeth, I know you are the bravest and strongest woman I have ever met, and you will weather this day with your indomitable courage." Darcy paused, willing himself not to cry and further distress his beloved wife. "You are everything to me, and I love you with my whole heart." He took his wife's hand and kissed it.

"You should know by now that my courage rises with every attempt to intimidate me. I love you, William, and the next time you see me, I will be holding our little babe." They managed to smile at each other and Darcy leaned over and kissed his wife's forehead. "Elizabeth, I am so happy I had the good sense to marry you."

Elizabeth smiled at their ongoing teasing 'argument', "what about my good sense? Please go now so I can have our baby." Darcy left the room just as another pain caused Elizabeth to cry out in distress. He heard his wife's cries when he neared the staircase and had to grip the bannister to keep himself from rushing back to her bedside.

Darcy slowly walked downstairs and anxiously waited in the front hall for all the people he expected to arrive. Mr. Laurence and the midwife were the first to appear, quickly followed by Jane and then Sir Knighton. They were all shown his wife's chambers, and Darcy was walking toward the drawing room when he saw Georgiana rushing down the stairs. "Is it time? Is Elizabeth having the baby now? What can I do to help?"

"Yes, little one, it is time. Please wait with me in the drawing room. They will not allow me to stay with her and I am going mad not being by her side. I know she is in good hands, but I cannot think clearly until I know she and the baby are well."

Georgiana took her brother's arm and walked him into the drawing room. She rang for tea and refreshments; although she was very excited about the prospect of becoming an aunt, she knew she could best help Elizabeth by keeping her brother as calm as possible.

SEVERAL HOURS HAD PASSED SINCE DARCY HAD LEFT his wife's bedside and he was crazy with worry. He was pacing in front of the fireplace when he saw Mrs. Reynolds enter the drawing room. Georgiana instantly rose to her feet and went to join her brother. Before they could ask, Mrs. Reynolds put her hands out in a staying gesture, "there is nothing to report yet; Mrs. Darcy is doing well and is being well cared for. As soon as I have more news, I will return but I wanted you to know that everything is proceeding as it should." Georgiana looked to her brother to respond but she saw he was nervously running his hand through his hair.

"Thank you, Mrs. Reynolds, please tell Mrs. Darcy that we are sending her all our love."

"Of course, Miss Georgiana, I will be happy to convey your message," the housekeeper said as she exited the drawing room and walked back upstairs.

He looked at his sister, "thank you, Georgie, for saying the right words. I am unable to think clearly right now. When did my little sister become so poised and mature?" Darcy leaned over and kissed the top of her head. "To be waiting down here while Elizabeth is enduring so much upstairs is one of the most difficult things I have ever done."

"We must be strong for Lizzy. Would you like me to play the pianoforte for you?"

"Yes, that is an excellent suggestion. I am grateful for the distraction."

GEORGIANA PLAYED FOR MORE THAN AN HOUR AND then she and her brother attempted to distract themselves with books. They pretended to be reading for another hour or more when Mrs. Reynolds finally entered the room. Darcy and Georgiana both jumped to their feet and were greeted with a big smile on the housekeeper's face. "Mr. Darcy, you may go up and see Mrs. Darcy now."

"Is she well, Mrs. Reynolds? And the baby?" Mrs. Reynolds did not answer but she continued smiling and motioned that Darcy should move toward the staircase.

He ran up the stairs two at a time and knocked gently on his wife's door. Several people at once said, "Come in!"

When he entered his wife's chambers, he saw Jane seated next to her sister on the bed. She was washing Elizabeth's face with a damp cloth and pushing back some of the many curls which were plastered to her cheeks and forehead. As soon as she saw Darcy, Jane rose and walked toward him. "Congratulations, William."

Darcy could not see or hear anything except his smiling wife and the tiny bundle she held in her arms. "Will you not come in, Papa, and meet your son?"

"My son," Darcy whispered as he walked toward the bed without seeing anything or anyone but his wife and child. When he reached the bedside, he saw that his wife was smiling, and her cheeks were rosy. "Are you well, my love? You look so beautiful and we have a son? A healthy baby?"

"Yes, William, with all these people here to help me, how could you expect anything else?" His heart soared at his wife's teasing words. He sat down next to her and put his arm around her shoulders. He kissed her head and leaned over to see his son.

"Would you like to hold him?"

"I am afraid. I mean, I am afraid I do not know what to do."

Sir Knighton heard Darcy's reply and gently took the baby from Elizabeth's arms. "It is very simple, Mr. Darcy. Always make sure you are supporting the baby's head and his rear end, and you will do well." Darcy rose and accepted the small bundle that Sir Knighton gently placed in his arms. He looked at the baby's face and saw that his son had his wife's beautiful dark curly hair and full lips; the baby briefly opened his eyes and looked up at his father.

"He is so beautiful. He looks so much like you, except his eyes are blue."

"I am sure Sir Knighton and Mr. Laurence will agree that most babies are born with blue eyes," Jane said as she smiled. "Maddie has the biggest brown eyes now but when she was born, her eyes were the same color as her cousin's. May I ask if my new nephew has a name?"

"His name is Bennet George Darcy," he said as he smiled at his wife.

"I believe that is a very fine name and I know our Papa will be very pleased," Jane smiled.

Sir Knighton stepped forward to speak to the Darcys. "I am a proponent of the modern view that believes that the best way to help Mrs. Darcy recover is to keep her chambers very clean. Open the drapes and even the windows for a few minutes every day; some fresh air is very healthy for everyone, but Mrs. Darcy should not do anything strenuous for at least the next month."

The accoucheur looked at the new mother, "when you are comfortable doing so, you may walk around your chambers or even to the nursery, but you should always be accompanied by your maid or your husband. I will examine you again tomorrow and I will return to Pemberley in a month's time to check on your recovery."

Mrs. Reynolds heard what Sir Knighton said and then added, "Mr. Darcy, if there is nothing else, I believe it is time for us to leave," she knew her master and mistress well enough to know they would prefer to be alone at this special time. She pointed her arm toward the door, "if you will all follow me; there are refreshments awaiting you in the drawing room." She turned toward the bed and said, "I will send Miss Georgiana up in a few minutes."

Jane went to her sister's side and kissed her forehead. "Bennet is a beautiful boy and I am so happy you wanted me to be with you today. I will send a note to Charles telling him the good news."

"Thank you, Jane. You made Bennet's birth so much easier for me. Just having you beside me gave me the confidence that I could do whatever was necessary."

The sisters embraced before Jane and everyone else exited the room.

Mrs. Reynolds stood at the door, "I would like to add my most sincere congratulations on Master Bennet's birth."

"Thank you, Mrs. Reynolds, for all your help today," Darcy said as he smiled at Pemberley's longtime housekeeper. Darcy sat at Elizabeth's bedside and put his arm around her shoulders. He looked into her eyes and quietly said, *"My bounty is as boundless as the sea, my love as deep; the more I give to thee, the more I have, for both are boundless."* He leaned over to kiss his wife and then he kissed his son who he gently held in his arms. They sat quietly, reflecting on the blessings they had received.

Elizabeth said quietly, "I never knew I could feel such joy. When you walked into Jane's drawing room last year, I thought my heart would burst with the happiness of knowing that you were alive. Being here, the three of us together, my heart is truly full. I told you on our first anniversary that our wedding day was the happiest day of my life. I hope you will not mind that I no longer feel that way; today my heart is so full of happiness and gratitude. We love each other and we have a beautiful baby boy; what more could anyone ask for?"

"I feel the same way you do, my love. When I walked in here and saw you holding the baby, my heart felt like it would jump out of my chest." They were smiling at each other when they heard knock on the door. “Come in, Georgie,” she said as her sister shyly walked into the room. “Come in and greet your nephew.”

“Oh Lizzy, I am so happy! I can see that you and the baby are well. Have you decided what to call him? Not Fitzwilliam, I hope,” Georgiana said with a laugh. “That name is much too much for a little baby!”

They joined Georgiana in her laughter and Elizabeth said, “Aunt Georgiana, please meet your nephew, Bennet George Darcy.”

“Bennet, I love that name and you followed the Fitzwilliam family tradition of naming the first son the maiden name of the mother. And George for our father; William, our parents would have been so pleased,” Georgiana said with tears in her eyes.

“Georgie, when we were reunited last summer, I expressed my sorrow at never knowing the wonderful people who brought you and William into the world. Your brother told me then that he felt your parents were always looking down and watching over you both. He said that they were his guardian angels and helped him recover from his terrible wounds.” Elizabeth and Darcy looked at each other remembering the happiness of the day they renewed their commitment to each other. “I told him when I accepted his proposal that your parents were now going to have to look after me, as well.

Now, they will also have to help us watch over Bennet."

Elizabeth looked at Georgiana and William and they all had tears in their eyes; tears of gratitude, tears of joy and tears of sadness for the two people who would never meet their precious grandson. Darcy smiled and nodded in agreement with his wife and then he stood up, so his sister could see her little nephew.

"He is so small, but he is the most beautiful baby I have ever seen! I will not linger, I know Lizzy must be very tired. I love you both and our new little baby, shall we call him Ben or Bennet? I am so happy you are both well; the halls of Pemberley will once again be filled with the sound of a baby's laughter." Georgiana reached across the bed and embraced Elizabeth before exiting the room.

When they were once again alone, Darcy said, "thank you for saying what you did about my parents. Georgiana was so young when they both died and has so few memories of them. I know she was happy to hear your words about them always watching over us." Darcy paused, his mind lost in his memories of his parents.

"Georgiana asked a good question; shall we call him Bennet or Ben ?

"Which do you prefer, Mama? His name is Bennet but is that too serious for a little baby? Of course, it is not as serious as Fitzwilliam!" The new parents smiled until Bennet began to stir, and Darcy said, "we can discuss it later. Elizabeth, are you truly feeling well?"

"I am incandescently happy, but I am tired. Bennet began announcing his desire to be born shortly after we went to bed. I spent most of last night in the chair you found me in this morning, gently rubbing my stomach. I did not wish to awaken the entire house until it was absolutely necessary. I knew everyone would need their rest before the baby made his entrance into the world," Elizabeth said and then added, "if you will excuse me, Papa, I believe I could use some rest."

"You know I love you very much, Mrs. Darcy."

"Mr. Darcy, your secret is safe with me." Elizabeth caressed his cheek as Darcy kissed his wife tenderly before she closed her eyes. He brought his son to the nursery and kissed his child before handing him to his nurse. He saw Hannah in the hallway and Darcy asked her to sit by his wife's bedside as she slept. As he walked downstairs to thank all the people who helped Elizabeth give birth to his son, all his fears of the past months were gone, and he felt as if he was walking on air.

DARCY SENT AN EXPRESS ANNOUNCING BENNET'S BIRTH to the residents of Longbourn. He did not like telling a lie, but knew his wife would not have fared as well as she had if her mother had been present. He assured his in-laws that although the baby was born early, the doctor assured them he was a very healthy little boy.

CHAPTER 9

At Rosings, Richard was delighted to receive a letter announcing the birth of Bennet George Darcy. Now that most of his estate responsibilities had been taken care of, Richard began to think ahead. He wondered if Lady Emily would be joining her brother at any of the Darcy's Christmastide festivities. *If she is still in Derbyshire and comes to Pemberley, what should I say to her? She did not seem very receptive to my attention when we were together in September. I know I am hoping that she will be there. Will she dance with me or will she still be dressed in widow's weeds for a husband everyone knew she never loved? Dare I tell her about my feelings? I think about her every night. I dream we are happily married and surrounded by laughing children. Richard, you are jumping ahead! She has most likely moved on from acting as her brother's hostess and, if she is there, will she give us a chance to get to know each other better? Could she ever have feelings for a grumpy old soldier?*

After the baby arrived, Darcy debated with himself about whether or not he should notify his Aunt Catherine of Bennet's birth. He had never told his wife the truth about his Aunt Catherine's feelings about their marriage. At the time, Darcy told her that his aunt was not feeling well and could not travel from London for the wedding. He felt his wife need not know that his aunt continued to spew her venom and hatred of Elizabeth to anyone who would listen. Aunt Catherine even blamed their marriage for the premature death of her daughter. She neglected to remember that Anne died long before their wedding, at a time when everyone, save Richard, thought Darcy was dead. The memory of her vitriolic rantings about Elizabeth after receiving their wedding invitation was still fresh in his mind. However, he reminded himself that Lady Catherine was his mother's older sister and he decided to write to her announcing the happy news of Bennet's birth.

The following week, his letter was returned to him unopened. Darcy knew then that he would most likely never see or hear from his aunt again and he quickly made peace with the idea. Georgiana would be making her debut into London society in a few months and he was happy to know that his Aunt Catherine would have no role in the occasion. When they returned to London, he would instruct his footmen to do anything necessary to prevent Lady

Catherine from entering Darcy House at any time. He would never allow his aunt to impose herself on his wife, sister or child. He would do whatever was necessary to keep Elizabeth and Georgiana away from the vile words of Lady Catherine. He threw the unopened letter into the fire and smiled contentedly. He had a wife he adored, a beautiful healthy baby and a sister who was growing into a young woman he was proud of.

THE DARCYS WERE OVER THE MOON WITH HAPPINESS. Bennet was growing well and was a sweet, even tempered baby who had all the adults in the house catering to his every need. Elizabeth was recovering well from the birth but did not resist when her husband insisted that she rest whenever Bennet was napping.

Sir Knighton returned to Derbyshire a month after Bennet's birth. After his examination, he assured the Darcys that Elizabeth was recovering well but needed to restrict her activities to within the house for several more weeks. "Please notify me if there are any setbacks in your progress. I will stop in Lambton and speak with Mr. Laurence about my findings today. I congratulate you both; your son is growing well and is a beautiful, healthy boy."

"Thank you, Sir Knighton. I really have no choice but to do as you ask; my husband watches me like a hawk." Elizabeth smiled at her husband, whose face had gotten a little red.

"Your husband is very concerned for your well-being and I wish every husband behaved as such. Good day and I wish you both the best of luck with your son.

AFTER DARCY RETURNED FROM ESCORTING SIR Knighton to his carriage, he walked with Elizabeth to the nursery. As they were standing over their son's cradle watching him sleep, Darcy said quietly, "I heard from my Aunt Catherine yesterday."

"Did she congratulate you on the birth of your son?"

"Not exactly." Darcy paused, trying to decide how much he should reveal to his wife. "I never told you about the letter she sent me after she received our wedding invitation."

"I seem to recall that you told me that she was not feeling well and could not travel to Derbyshire."

"That was not the reason she did not attend. I had not wished to upset you with the truth right before the wedding. There is no reason to repeat any of the vitriol she spewed in her letter. In fact, I never read all of it; after the first few paragraphs I was so disgusted, I threw it into the fire."

"Why have you chosen to speak of her today?"

"I debated whether or not to send her a note announcing Ben's birth. In the end, I told myself that she is my mother's older sister and should be given the respect due her."

"How did she react to our wonderful news?"

"She returned my letter to me, unopened. I threw that letter into the fire as well. I pray that we shall never see or hear from Lady Catherine again."

"Can you be happy with that declaration?"

"When I saw the unopened letter, I was initially hurt by her callousness. After I thought about it for a few hours, I realized that I was totally at peace with the decision of her making. Elizabeth, I have everything I have ever dreamed about. You and Ben are all I will ever need for my happiness. I will never allow anyone to interfere with our family."

"I think you have handled the situation very well. I cannot think of any other reaction that would have been more satisfactory." They kissed briefly and then smiled down at their sleeping son. They quietly left the nursery walking hand in hand.

EARLY IN DECEMBER, ELIZABETH, DARCY, GEORGIANA and Mrs. Reynolds walked the short distance to the Pemberley Chapel for the ceremony of Thanksgiving. The Darcys had asked Mr. Carter to preside at the service; he came to the Pemberley Chapel rather than requiring Mrs. Darcy to travel. Mr. Carter spoke beautifully about the joys of motherhood and the gratitude they all felt that Elizabeth and Bennet were well. As the rite required, Elizabeth responded with her own prayer of thanks which brought everyone in the chapel to tears. After thanking Mr. Carter for his services, the Darcys invited him to join them for lunch. "I am grateful for the invitation, but I have promised to visit some of my parishioners today. I do look forward to seeing you all soon." After thanking Mr. Carter again, the happy group began walking the short distance back to the house.

"Now that you have been churched, my dear wife, I hope you will not take it upon yourself to travel from our home or take on too much while preparing for our upcoming guests."

"I appreciate your care, my dearest husband, and I promise to stay very close to home. I will gladly share my hostessing responsibilities with our very competent staff. Mrs. Reynolds and I have already spoken about whom we expect to stay and what their needs will be. Does that make you happy, Mr. Darcy?"

"I would be a lot happier if your words were sincere." All three women laughed at Darcy's ever-present concern for his wife's well-being. "Remember what Sir Knighton said, you should be happy to have such a concerned husband."

"I will be very happy to help Lizzy and Mrs. Reynolds prepare for our guests' arrival. I will keep a close watch out that my sister does not do too much."

"Thank you, Georgie, I hope your words are as sincere as my wife's." They all smiled as Darcy lifted his wife's hand and placed a kiss on her glove.

As they approached the house, Roberts approached them and bowed. "Excuse me, ma'am. Mr. Darcy told me you would like to speak to me."

Elizabeth walked toward him and placed her hand on his arm. "Roberts, I wanted to thank you myself for risking your life so Sanders could be captured. I will always be in your debt. Please let me or Mr. Darcy know if there is anything we can do for you."

"I was happy to help you, ma'am. If you will excuse me, I should get back to work." Roberts bowed and walked back toward the stables.

Elizabeth looked at her husband, "I suppose you arranged this meeting?"

"I thought he would feel less uncomfortable if you met with others around."

"Our meeting today was just what I hoped for. Thank you for arranging it."

Darcy bowed to his wife. "Madam, I am at your service." Everyone smiled and continue the short walk to the manor house.

THE DARCYS HAD INVITED THE BENNETS AND ALL THEIR daughters, the Bingleys, the Gardiners and the Fitzwilliams to Pemberley for Christmas. They encouraged their guests to arrive as early in the month as possible; they worried that foul weather could impede or prevent their journeys. Lydia Bennet was traveling with her parents; she was home for the festive season from the boarding school her new brother was happy to pay for. Darcy and Elizabeth knew the youngest Bennet sister desperately lacked an education and the knowledge of how to behave like a lady. They were anxious to see if there was any improvement in Lydia's behavior.

Jane, Charles and Maddie Bingley were planning to journey from their nearby estate. Two of Elizabeth's sisters were unable to attend; Catherine, who was now married to Lord Winthrope, was anticipating the imminent birth of their first child. She and her husband were unwilling to venture away from home for any reason. Her sister, Mary, who had never believed in participating in what she considered to be frivolous activities, wrote that she saw no reason to travel all the way to Derbyshire in the winter to celebrate the birth of Jesus. She was too busy helping her husband in his law practice and completing her charity work in time for all the Christmas donations to be distributed.

In addition to Christmas dinner, the Darcys were

planning a a big party on Boxing Day. Everyone was looking forward to the festivities which promised to include a Yule log, dancing, food, games for the children and gift baskets for all of Pemberley's tenants.

Caroline Bingley had unexpectedly arrived at Birchwood Manor a week before Christmas. After her stay in Derbyshire and attending the Harvest Ball, she had not stopped thinking about Mr. Carter when she returned to the Hursts' townhouse in London. Although completely untrue, Caroline told the Hursts that she had received an invitation to visit the Bingleys and return to Birchwood Manor for the festive season. The Hursts welcomed the news and looked forward to the quiet that would soon pervade their home in Caroline's absence.

After arriving in Derbyshire, she expressed her willingness to accompany the Bingleys to all of the Darcy's celebrations. She was secretly looking forward to seeing Mr. Carter again. Jane sent a note apprising Elizabeth that Caroline was again their houseguest and would be attending all the festivities at Pemberley. She apologized for Caroline's impulsive behavior and hoped there was room to accommodate another guest. Elizabeth sent word to her sister that one more guest would be no hardship and would be welcomed as a member of the family.

The Darcys' guests slowly began to arrive over the weeks leading up to Christmas and were easily accommodated in Pemberley's numerous guest suites. They were all looking forward to attending the Christmas morning service followed by a sumptuous Christmas dinner.

By the week before the holiday, Pemberley was full of happy family members and friends, eager to spend time getting to know each other and celebrating the joyous holidays together. Everyone had arrived in time to celebrate Bennet's christening and all the Christmas festivities. Mrs. Bennet was frequently overheard saying that she could not understand how the baby, who was supposedly born so early, had already grown so much.

The day before their child's christening, Elizabeth and Darcy waited in the grand entrance hall of Pemberley while awaiting their final guests to arrive. When the Bingleys' carriage pulled to a stop, the Darcys warmly greeted Jane, Charles and Maddie and welcomed Caroline with as much sincerity as possible.

~

THE NEXT DAY, THE DARCYS AND ALL THEIR GUESTS walked the short distance to the Pemberley Chapel to witness the christening of Bennet George Darcy. Jane and Charles were asked to be Bennet's godparents and they were both very honored to consent.

Caroline entered the Chapel and when she sat beside

Jane, she immediately saw that Mr. Carter was already in the Church. She found it difficult to stop looking at him. While Mr. Carter officiated, Caroline's heart was beating rapidly and her cheeks were red. Jane had been watching her sister's face and thought, *she must be half in love with him already. I have never seen her react to a man as she is now. Peter Carter is a compassionate man; would he have any desire to court Caroline if he knew the truth about her less-than-caring behavior?*

Darcy and Elizabeth stood beside Jane and Charles and each was smiling with joy at this dear child in their arms. Bennet looked wonderful in his christening gown, a Darcy heirloom; swaddled in a beautiful christening blanket which had been lovingly embroidered for this important day by his Aunt Georgiana and Mrs. Annesley. Jane was holding Bennet as he slept peacefully until Mr. Carter sprinkled some holy water on his head and he woke up screaming. The chapel was full of the Darcys' family and closest friends and even while listening to the loud wails of the Darcy heir, joy and gratitude was felt by everyone in attendance.

Darcy offered a few words of his own. "Our son bears the name of his mother's family. A family I thank every day for creating my son's mother." Both Mr. and Mrs. Bennet were smiling with tears in their eyes as Darcy spoke. "His other name is the name of.." Darcy's speech faltered, and Elizabeth walked closer to her husband and took his hand in hers.

There were tears in his eyes as he continued, "he bears the name of my dearest father. He and my dear mother are Bennet's guardian angels and will help us protect our precious child." Darcy's words brought happy tears to the eyes of his family and Mr. Carter then concluded the service. After everyone returned to the manor house, a bountiful meal was planned to celebrate Bennet's christening, although the guest of honor was not in attendance.

On December twenty third, most of Pemberley's guests joined Elizabeth and Georgiana as they walked the paths that had been cleared of the fresh snow. They collected holly, ivy, and other greenery which Elizabeth and Georgiana wanted to use when they decorated the house. Mrs. Reynolds supervised the group as they all participated in adorning the house with the garlands and greenery they had gathered. They strung apples, twigs and ribbons to decorate the holly bough that would hang from the ceiling in the main drawing room.

The women guests also gathered herbs from the still room and created sachets which were hung throughout the house and their fragrant aromas were enjoyed by all. Jane brought orange pomanders from Mrs. Wilson, their cook at Birchwood Manor. It was during Elizabeth's first Christmas living with the Bingleys, shortly after she learned of Darcy's "death", that Birchwood's cook explained that the cloves in the orange pomanders symbolized undying love. The following year, Mrs. Wilson gifted the newly married Mrs. Darcy with a bag of cloves shortly after the Darcys returned from their wedding trip. Rather than keep the spice in the kitchen, Elizabeth always felt the cloves belonged in her bedroom. She kept the spice in a drawer with her handkerchiefs, where she enjoyed their scent and they served as a reminder of the undying love she felt for her husband.

Georgiana was put in charge of the parlor games for all of Pemberley's guests and kept them entertained after dinner. She planned word games, chess tournaments; organized games of whist and Loo and she orchestrated a very challenging scavenger hunt. On other nights, many of the ladies played the pianoforte and all their guests joined in singing Christmas songs. Every evening, their guests climbed the stairs to their rooms with smiles on their faces.

Elizabeth collected some mistletoe to hang near the entrance to the drawing room, but Mrs. Reynolds quietly informed her mistress that the tradition of kissing under this particular plant should remain below stairs in the servants' quarters. Elizabeth warmly thanked Mrs. Reynolds from saving her from making a social *faux pas*.

~

When they were alone in their chambers later that night, Darcy said, "I have something for you, Mrs. Darcy," and removed a sprig of mistletoe from his pocket and held it over Elizabeth's head.

"Mr. Darcy, I am surprised at you. Mrs. Reynolds told me that kissing under the mistletoe was not appropriate for people of our elevated social standing," she teased.

"I agree that we should not have our guests standing under the mistletoe and kissing. It is just not acceptable for such exalted members of the *ton*," Darcy said jokingly.

"And yet, here you are, holding some mistletoe over my head in the expectation I will kiss you."

"Will you not kiss your husband, madam?" Darcy teased as he gathered his wife into his arms and kissed her passionately.

"Well, maybe just this once, sir!" Elizabeth giggled as she grabbed the mistletoe from her husband. She ran toward the bed and raised the plant over her head as she turned to welcome her husband into her warm embrace.

CHAPTER 10

On Christmas morning, Darcy and Elizabeth went to see Bennet in the nursery before joining their guests for breakfast. Darcy had whittled a small wooden horse for his little boy, who was much too young to understand what the gift was for. Elizabeth presented her son with a new blanket on which she had embroidered his name and the date of his birth. Before leaving for services, the family presented simple gifts to all the children in attendance.

Caroline attended Christmas services at the Kympton Church along with the Darcys, their other guests and most of the members of the parish. She was surprised by the warm feelings she, once again, felt toward the man standing at the pulpit. Jane watched Caroline during the service, and she noticed that her sister never took her eyes off the vicar. *Maybe she does have real feelings for him. She normally judges people solely by their standing in the ton. The real question is whether or not Mr. Carter is attracted to a well-known social climber?*

Richard saw Lady Emily standing in one of the front pews and suddenly felt that his valet had tied his cravat too tightly. She was greeting her brother's parishioners as they made their way to their seats. When she looked up and saw Richard, she briefly smiled at him before turning to speak to someone else.

As he began his first Christmas service in Derbyshire, the congregation could feel that Mr. Carter's words reflected the caring and generous nature of the man whose sermon was all about the true meaning of Christmas. "Today we come together to celebrate the birth of baby Jesus. Gratitude, hope, faith and charity are the true meaning of this joyous holiday; not just for today, but for the lives we live every day of the year."

Jane sat beside Caroline and as she listened to Mr. Carter, she could see her sister was breathing quickly, and her face was turning red. *If she had to stand at this moment, I do not believe her legs would hold her. What has this man done to her? Does she have real affection for Peter Carter? That is inconceivable! Does she love him? Does she want to marry him? Could she ever give up her life of luxury in the ton for the life of being married to a country vicar? I must speak to her about her emotions. I may not tell her what she wants to hear but she knows I would never lie to her. She should spend more time with Mr.*

Carter and determine her true feelings. Does he like her? Can he possibly envision Caroline as a vicar's wife? What if her sentiments are not reciprocated? I hope she knows what she wants. It is time I spoke to Charles about this.

By the time the service had ended, Jane could see that Caroline had finally come to her senses; the Bingleys joined the congregation as everyone was slowly departing the church. As she made her way to the doorway, Caroline overheard many people commenting on Mr. Carter's meaningful sermon. They all told him how happy they were that Mr. Darcy had granted him the living at Kympton. *And another thing, Mr. Carter lives on the largesse of Mr. Darcy. Could Caroline live her life beholden to the Darcys? She had worked tirelessly to make Darcy her husband and never had a kind thing to say about Elizabeth.*

As she was leaving the church, Caroline stopped and thanked the vicar for his meaningful words. Jane was standing directly behind her and overheard Caroline's compliment. *I have never heard her compliment anyone, much less a man who could not possibly be seen as a potential suitor.* Mr. Carter took her hand and bowed over it and then he thanked Caroline for her kind words. He told her that he and his sister were looking forward to joining the Darcys for Christmas dinner later that day.

Richard looked for Lady Emily as everyone was leaving the church. There were so many people in the aisles that it was difficult to see past the person in front of you and Richard was disappointed that he did not have a chance to speak to her. The Darcys had assured him that Mr. Carter and Lady Emily had both said they were looking forward to enjoying Christmas dinner at Pemberley. Darcy had told his cousin that they also planned to attend tomorrow's Boxing Day festivities and Richard would have many opportunities to speak to Lady Emily. He was hoping to spend time with her before dinner was served and prayed that they would be seated near each other for the festive meal.

Mr. Carter and Lady Emily arrived at Pemberley while the Darcys' guests were gathered in the drawing room, partaking of mulled cider. Darcy escorted the Carters around the room and introduced them to his family and friends. When the group came near the Fitzwilliams, Richard saw his mother quickly appraise Lady Emily and smile. Before any conversation could begin, everyone was called into the grand dining room.

Elizabeth had supervised the table decor and had arranged the seating carefully. She attempted to seat their guests in a way that might encourage the affections of at least one young couple who seemed to be attracted to one another. Darcy had told her about Richard's feelings, and she hoped that spending

Christmas at Pemberley might help their cousin get to know Lady Emily better.

Elizabeth had no idea where to place Caroline, so she decided that seating her next to Peter Carter might minimize her caustic remarks. Elizabeth remembered all too clearly the verbal barbs that Caroline aimed at her throughout the Bingleys' stay in Hertfordshire. She had noticed that Caroline had been on her best behavior since arriving unexpectedly for the Harvest Ball, but she did not yet trust her to behave as a welcome guest should.

Caroline was seated to Peter Carter's right and she silently thanked Mrs. Darcy for placing her there. She felt shy and wracked her brain trying to find a topic that she and Mr. Carter could discuss. Jane sat to the vicar's left and she tried not to be too obvious as she attempted to overhear their conversation. Again, Caroline noticed that he was very well dressed. To her relief, Mr. Carter began the conversation, "Miss Bingley, will you remain in Derbyshire long?"

"My plans are not set, and I am enjoying my stay with my brother and Jane. I normally spend the entire Season in Town, but I am very happy here and I believe I will remain for at least a few more weeks."

"I am happy to hear that." Mr. Carter quickly smiled at his dinner companion and then turned his attention to his plate. Jane was certain she heard him say that he was happy Caroline would remain in Derbyshire. *What did he mean by that? Does Mr. Carter have feelings for my sister? What can I do to encourage her to spend more time with him?*

"Mr. Carter, I cannot help but notice your clothes." The words escaped her mouth before she could control her tongue.

"My clothes, Miss Bingley?"

Jane could not believe what Caroline just said. *Why would she say such a thing to someone she hardly knows? I know she attended the best finishing schools, but she certainly did not learn to ask that type of question there!*

"I recognize the work of one of London's foremost haberdashers. My brother, Charles, and my brother in law often use the same store. I thought a man of God would be dressed more simply."

"You are very observant, madam. The truth is, I am dressed this way because my mother will not take 'no' for an answer. Every season she has the tailor send me new clothes in the latest styles despite my repeated pleas to allow me to make my own sartorial decisions. I should be angry about it, but my parishioners are benefitting from my mother's objective of having a well-dressed son despite my protestations."

"I do not understand how your new wardrobe benefits your congregation."

"When my new garments arrive, I donate all my old clothes to my worshippers. If you return to my parish, you might notice some of the tenant farmers wearing an unusually stylish jacket or waistcoat."

"How very generous of you, Mr. Carter."

"Thank you for saying that, Miss Bingley, but I do not think of it as being generous, merely doing my Christian duty. What happens to your gowns when they are no longer the latest fashion in Town?"

"I am embarrassed to say that I do not know. My maid removes them from my closet and where they go from there, I cannot say."

"I would venture to guess that your maid gives them to her family or perhaps she sells them to have a little extra money."

"I thank you for asking that question. I will look into the matter as soon as I speak to my maid later this evening. I will make sure my old dresses are donated to the local church, so another woman can enjoy wearing them."

"How very generous of you, Miss Bingley."

Caroline paused and looked down at her hands while she gathered her thoughts. "Mr. Carter, please accept my apology for asking about your clothes. I noticed how well dressed you were when we met in September. I confess that I am too accustomed to judging people by the quality of their clothing instead of getting to know someone for who they are. I hope you will forgive me." Jane was smiling as she heard her sister apologize. *Perhaps meeting Mr. Carter has had a positive effect on Caroline. There is always hope!*

"There is nothing to forgive. I admit that I was often embarrassed to wear such expensive clothes when many of my parishioners have so little. As soon as I began donating them to the neediest of my flock, they did not seem to mind that their spiritual leader was a bit of a Beau Brummell." They smiled and both felt that they knew each other better. Jane was happily surprised by the conversation that had just transpired next to her. *He has told her so much about himself and I believe she will make sure her old dresses are donated. This man has had a profound effect on her. Who is Caroline becoming? She is not the same woman she was six months ago.*

Caroline was also deep in thought, *before meeting Peter Carter, I never thought about what happened to my old things nor did I care. If someone was not dressed in the latest fashions, I could not be bothered to speak with them. What is happening to me? Do I have feelings for Mr. Carter and have these feelings changed the person I am? If I am not the social climbing Caroline Bingley, who am I?* Caroline smiled at the positive changes in herself and began to enjoy Christmas dinner. She took small bites of the Christmas goose and braised vegetables but was so distracted by Peter Carter's presence she could not enjoy the food on her plate.

ON THE OTHER SIDE OF THE TABLE, RICHARD WAS SEATED

next to Lady Emily. *I see Lizzy and Darcy are trying to play matchmakers. Well, they will get no complaint from me.* "Lady Emily, are you enjoying your time in Derbyshire?"

"Yes, I have grown to appreciate the weather here and I have always been close to my brother, Peter. Although he is very busy taking care of his congregants, for the first time in a very long while we have had the opportunity to have many meaningful discussions."

"May I presume to ask what you speak about?"

"Life, love, families; the usual after-dinner conversations." Lady Emily smiled at Richard with affection before turning her eyes to the food before her. Once again, Richard felt his cravat tightening on his neck. *I will dismiss Barton in the morning! Is the man trying to strangle me? What did Lady Emily's smile mean? Does she feel affection for me? I must spend more time with her before declaring myself. Declaring myself? I do not know if I will ever see her again. Richard, do not think that way! I do not know when, but I must see her again. I refuse to let Emily slip out of my life!*

"Mrs. Covington's roast lamb has always been a favorite of mine. She has catered to my preferences since she came to Pemberley many years ago and I came here during my holidays from school. She failed to realize that anything she put before me was far better than any food served at school Her plum pudding is not to be missed!"

"Thank you for the suggestions. Ginger bread has always been my favorite Christmas dessert. I wonder if it will be served this evening?"

"Based on my past holidays at Pemberley, I believe you will not have to wait long before ginger bread is before you." Emily smiled at Richard's comment and returned to her meal.

Elizabeth had been a bit nervous about hosting so many people since this was her first Christmas dinner in the large dining room. She smiled as she looked around the table and saw everyone enjoying their meal. When the last dessert was finished, all the guests praised the dishes that were served and Elizabeth's remarkable hostessing skills.

Later that evening, Darcy knocked on the door of his wife's chambers and entered with his hands behind his back. It was obvious to Elizabeth that he was unsuccessfully trying to conceal the fact that he was holding a very large box. "What are you attempting to hide from me?"

"I suppose I am being a bit obvious, but before we get to it, I must thank you for tonight. Everything was just perfect and it appeared as if you have been planning large festive meals your whole life." They both laughed. "Now, back to whatever you think I am holding behind me. I know we said that only the children would receive gifts but when I saw this, I knew you must have it."

"I really should not accept it since we agreed to no gifts, but my curiosity has been piqued and I am eagerly awaiting to see what is inside." Darcy sat beside his wife on the edge of her bed and watched her face react to the contents of the box. "Oh, William, this is the most wonderful gift I have ever received. But how?" Elizabeth was overcome with emotion as she held up a beautiful framed painting of Longbourn, her childhood home.

"I wrote to an artist I know in London and commissioned the painting. Then, I wrote to Mr. Bennet and asked his permission to have Mr. Townsend set up his easel on the drive so he could best capture the house in the afternoon light. Do you like it? I thought you would enjoy hanging it here in your bed chamber to look upon whenever you wish."

Elizabeth placed her hands around her husband's neck and pulled him close enough to kiss. "It is wonderful. I will hang it over my fireplace so I can see it every morning when I wake up. I cannot thank you enough for this thoughtful gift." Darcy was pleased that he had surprised his wife and was delighted with her reaction. "However, you are not the only one who did not adhere to our *no gifts* policy. Now, where did I put it?" Elizabeth was tapping her fingers to her lips pretending she could not remember where she had put her husband's present. "Oh, yes, here it is under the bed." Elizabeth presented Darcy with a box nearly as big as his gift to her.

"Whatever this is, you really should not have." They both laughed. Darcy opened the box and inside was a beautifully embroidered waistcoat. He could see the hundreds of tiny stitches which enhanced the beautiful fabric. "You have been so busy caring for Bennet, organizing everything for our guests and *supposedly* resting, I cannot imagine how you found the time to work on this. You are my dearest, most wonderful wife and I thank you from the bottom of my heart. I will wear it tomorrow at the Yuletide party and show everyone how clever I was to have the good sense to make you my wife."

Elizabeth teased her husband, "there you go again, what about my good sense?" Darcy embraced Elizabeth and as they began to kiss, they knew that their love for each other was, without question, the greatest gift of all.

CHAPTER 11

DECEMBER 1813

Mrs. Reynolds and Elizabeth spent many hours working together while planning for the Boxing Day party. The housekeeper told her as much as she remembered from the Boxing Day celebrations held at Pemberley when both of Darcy's parents were alive. Together they read through all the notes in the housekeeper's office and decided that one of the planned highlights would be the lighting of the Yule Log. The log had to be large enough to burn throughout the remainder of the festive days. Several footmen were needed to carry the Yule Log into the ballroom fireplace after it had been cut from one of the oldest trees in Pemberley's forest. The kindling from the last Yule Log was traditionally used to light this year's and, of course, Mrs. Reynolds knew exactly where the kindling from many years' past was kept in storage. She had always hoped that the Darcy family would once again celebrate Christmas as they once had. Before it was placed in the hearth, the adults laughed as many of the young children attempted to climb up on the Yule Log which was thought to bring them good luck.

When Mr. Carter arrived with his sister, Richard immediately noticed that Lady Emily was wearing a beautiful dark green gown. He assumed that she was finally out of mourning for her husband, yet when he approached her, she seemed more distant than she had been at Christmas dinner. He thought Boxing Day might hold some unknown significance to her and perhaps today's events reminded her of her unhappy marriage. He hoped that he would one day hear Lady Emily explain her behavior, but she demurred when Richard asked her to dance one of the holiday reels with him.

Georgiana organized games for the children, Oranges and Lemons, Pins, Battledore and Shuttlecock. Darcy and Elizabeth were delighted to see their dearest sister taking charge of all the little ones.

While the musicians were tuning their instruments, Darcy and Elizabeth stood in the center of the ballroom and welcomed their guests. "Welcome back to Pemberley! Mrs. Darcy and I are very happy that we are all together to celebrate this joyous season. It has been many years since we celebrated Christmastide together and let us pray that these celebrations will continue for many years to come. Cheers!" Darcy raised his glass, and everyone joined him in his toast. After he spoke, Elizabeth was given the honor of lighting the Yule Log, when the flames began to rise, everyone cheered again for the renewal of this Pemberley tradition.

When people approached Darcy to thank him for the party, he subconsciously rubbed the stitching on his new waistcoat; which prompted his guests to comment on the beauty of the needlework. Mr. Ward, one of Pemberley's longtime tenants approached Darcy and expressed his admiration for Darcy's beautifully embroidered garment.

"My lovely wife made this for me. I do not know where Mrs. Darcy found the time, but I treasure her kindness."

"We are all very happy about the woman you took as your wife, sir. She has visited us many times and is always very kind and generous to my family; I know the other tenants feel the same way. We are all very grateful for Mrs. Darcy." His host nodded and smiled in response, but he could not speak; his heart was overflowing with love for his amazing wife.

AS THE MUSICIANS WERE WARMING UP THEIR instruments, buffet tables were loaded with platters of cold meats, breads, cakes, biscuits and cider. The children were not permitted to sample the Yule Cake which was soaked in ale and only offered to the adults. Many small tables were scattered around the ballroom and were covered with simple cloths and centerpieces made from pine cones and berry branches.

Elizabeth noticed that Mr. Carter was dancing with Caroline and Richard was speaking with Lady Emily. *Perhaps I am better at matchmaking than I thought. I cannot see Caroline being attracted to a clergyman but none of William's friends would have ever expected him to marry someone like me. I suppose love is love and only time will tell if their feelings are real. She has been much more pleasant to be around. I have not seen her usual sneer or overheard her criticize anything in months!*

When the tenants departed, they were all handed gift baskets containing some cold meat, bread, a few potatoes, a slice of the Darcy family's Christmas plum cake, a sack of corn, some candy and some tea. Each gift basket also contained some candles and a few small presents for the children; skipping ropes for the boys and balls in the cup for the girls.

SEVERAL DAYS LATER, ELIZABETH AWOKE IN HER husband's arms and as she opened her eyes, she noticed that William had arranged to have her portrait of Longbourn hung on the wall above her fireplace. She stared at the portrait of her childhood home and admired how the morning light, coming in through the windows, enhanced the colors of the painting. *I am truly married to the kindest, most wonderful man in the world. For so long, I thought I*

would never feel joy again, and then William came back to me. She had tears in her eyes as she felt William awaken beside her.

"Good morning, my love." Darcy turned to kiss his wife, "Elizabeth, why you are crying? Are you unwell?" Darcy sat up and took her hands in his.

Elizabeth smiled at her husband and shook her head. "When I awoke, I saw the painting of Longbourn, and I began reminiscing about everything that has transpired in the past two and a half years. In that time, I went from happiness to utter heartbreak and now the overwhelming joy I feel every day."

"I am happy you like the painting, but I hope it does not continue to make you sad when you look at it. When I look at Longbourn, I see the home where my wonderful wife became the woman she is now, the woman I love with all my heart and always will."

"That is how I shall look at it as well. If I had not been happily walking Longbourn's fields, I would never have met you or gotten to know the wonderful person you are. You are correct, Longbourn is an important part of my current happiness and I thank you again for my cherished gift." Elizabeth turned in William's embrace and began kissing him. Their passion was quickly ignited and, on this morning, the Darcys were not present to greet their guests when they arrived in the breakfast room.

~

SHORTLY AFTER THE NEW YEAR, RICHARD GATHERED HIS courage and rode to Kympton to call on Lady Emily. After he was welcomed to the parsonage, Richard asked, "Lady Emily, would you care to join me for a walk? The weather is unusually mild for January and I know that I always enjoy the fresh air after spending so many days indoors." Mr. Carter did not wish to send one of the maids out into the cold weather, so he accompanied Richard and Lady Emily for propriety's sake.

While they were walking, the Carter siblings told Richard about growing up in Ipswich and several humorous stories that all siblings share. They spoke of past Christmas celebrations at their family's estate in Suffolk but did not mention Emily's parents or her marriage. They did not stay outside for long due to the temperature and when they neared the parsonage, Richard accepted their invitation to join them for tea. As it drew close to the time for his visit to end, a feeling of sadness overcame Richard as he stood to take his leave. He was sorry he would be separated from Lady Emily for the foreseeable future. "I thank you both for your kind hospitality. I have enjoyed spending time with you," He directed his gaze at the object of his affection, "and hope to see you both again soon. Lady Emily, are you planning to return to Town, or will you remain in Derbyshire?"

"My plans are not yet established. I will remain here until Twelfth Night and I will then decide what to do next. Safe travels, Mr. Fitzwilliam." Lady Emily curtsied, and Richard bowed before quickly leaving the parsonage. After his visit to Kympton, Richard decided it was time he returned to Rosings; there was nothing or no one keeping him in Derbyshire.

Once he was back in Kent, he knew in his heart that he was deeply in love with Lady Emily, but he was saddened to acknowledge his feelings were not reciprocated. Perhaps she was still emotionally fragile because of what her parents made her do and the very bad experience her marriage had been.

JANE INSISTED ON HOSTING THE FAMILY AT BIRCHWOOD Manor for their Twelfth Night Celebration. She knew her sister was already doing too much so soon after giving birth. By Twelfth Night, the Darcys had been entertaining most of the family for more than a month and Jane insisted on helping her sister by assuming all the planning for the celebration. "Elizabeth, Mama and Papa will stay at Birchwood for Twelfth Night and then leave to visit Catherine for a few days before departing for Longbourn. Please let me do this for you; after Twelfth Night you are soon to London and preparing for Georgiana's debut. Charles and I would like to establish some of our own holiday traditions, so perhaps hosting the Twelfth Night Ball can be our first." Elizabeth was inwardly relieved and readily accepted when Jane volunteered to host the event.

Elizabeth had enjoyed having a houseful of guests but was eager for everyone to depart. She was looking forward to spending more private time with Darcy, Bennet and Georgiana. In early January, the Darcys, Gardiners and the Bennets traveled to Birchwood Manor in a caravan of coaches. Everyone was delighted to see the lovely holiday décor planned by Jane and Caroline. On the night of their arrival, everyone was treated to a delicious festive dinner. After dining, all the guests were required to participate in the traditional taking down of all the Christmastide decorations. Charles and Darcy led the men out to a field in back of the house where a large fire had been lit. According to local legend, all the decorations must be burned before midnight in order to prevent any goblins from nearing anyone on the Bingley estate.

The following day, everyone enjoyed the Twelfth Night Ball where all the guests were expected to don masks and costumes. It took some serious late-night convincing by Elizabeth to garner the cooperation of her husband to such a scheme. He only agreed to wear a mask, no amount of "convincing" could motivate him to also agree to wearing a costume. Since it was a short trip to the Bingleys' estate and the Darcys would only be away for two days, he convinced his wife that Bennet was best left at home and she ultimately agreed with the decision. Maddie was too young to attend the party but the Gardiner children were invited to participate in the early hours of the dance; they merrily roamed around the ballroom in their colorful costumes and masks. The highlight of the night for the children was the presentation of the Twelfth Night Cake, which was beautifully decorated with elaborate sugar creations, gilded paper trimmings and delicious sweet icing.

Lady Emily and Mr. Carter attended the party, but initially, neither was seen dancing. Lady Emily tried not to be too obvious as she looked around the Bingley's ballroom searching for Richard and was disappointed not to see him. At the parsonage, he told her that he was returning to Kent the following day, but she hoped that he might have changed his plans. Mr. Carter spoke to his hosts and saw Miss Bingley directing the servants as to where she wanted the food to be served. He bowed before her and went into the ballroom to speak to some of the other guests. Caroline was saddened by his brusque greeting. *Why was he so cold to me? Is he angry at me for some reason? I will get to the bottom of this and I will not leave Derbyshire until I know whether or not Peter Carter has feelings for me! Oh, Caroline, why do you care? He is a poor country vicar and we can never have a romantic relationship. He is not wealthy and never will be. How could I ever maintain my standing in the ton if I was married to a vicar?*

Later in the evening, Peter Carter asked Caroline to dance and she happily accepted. When she placed her hand on his arm, she felt her heart race and she blushed. In the course of the dance, every time their hands touched, she felt a similar reaction. *Does Peter feel the same thrill when he touches me? Is his heart beating as quickly as mine?* She was disappointed when the set ended; he walked her back to her family, bowed and walked away. *Now what should I think? He asked me to dance but we had almost no conversation. If this is what falling in love feels like, I do not know if my heart can bear not being loved by Peter Carter.*

THE DAY AFTER THE BALL, THE GARDINERS LEFT Derbyshire for London and the Bennets were traveling to Winthrope Hall to visit Lady Catherine (nee Bennet) and her husband, Lord Winthrope. Mrs. Bennet could not be stopped from her loud expressions of happiness regarding the grandeur in which three of her daughters now lived. She was certain that now that her youngest child was learning how to be a real lady, only a most advantageous marriage would be acceptable. She was also overheard telling Lydia that she had enough stories to keep Lady Lucas and Aunt Phillips in awe for months.

As they walked to the waiting carriages outside Birchwood Manor, Elizabeth bade her father a sad farewell. Mr. Bennet turned to his daughter and took her hands in his. "Lizzy, I will not thank you and Darcy for your generous hospitality these many weeks. I do want to thank you for allowing me to enjoy the library at Pemberley to its fullest extent and even take some tomes with me." Mr. Bennet paused and brushed aside some tears.

"Papa, what is it? Have we upset you somehow? Would you rather not travel today and remain here with Jane or return to Pemberley?"

"No child, I wish to thank you for giving your old Papa the joy he never knew he could feel. I love Maddie and our precious little Bennet, and I am so grateful for the joy I see in your eyes."

"Papa, please promise to come back soon. Bennet and Maddie need their grandfather to teach them so many things. I am happier than I ever dreamed possible. My love for Darcy and now my son, grows every day. I will miss you, but we will stop at Longbourn for a few days on our way to London."

"I will look forward to that. Now, we must be off. I will write you when we reach Longbourn. I am looking forward to spending a great deal of time in my library. Your husband was generous enough to share a number of his favorite books with me. The good news is that Mrs. Bennet will most likely be gone for weeks, crowing about her time in Derbyshire and celebrating Christmas with the nobility." Elizabeth and her father both smiled as he kissed her cheek and entered the carriage for their trip.

CHAPTER 12

Several days after the Darcys were contentedly returned to the normal peace and quiet of Pemberley, Darcy awaited Elizabeth to return to her chambers after her last visit to the nursery for the night. When she entered their sitting room, he asked, "and how did you find our son, my dear? Much changed from our visit one hour ago?" Darcy enjoyed teasing his wife but silently admired what a wonderfully caring mother she was. He knew that many women of the *ton* left the upbringing of their children exclusively to nurses and nannies.

"Your son is sleeping soundly, and I kissed him goodnight from both of us."

"Elizabeth, I kissed Bennet goodnight an hour ago. Surely, you do not think I am remiss in my attentions to my child?" Darcy teased again.

"No, William, I know you are a wonderful father as you

are a wonderful husband and brother to Georgiana. It seems like so long since it has just been our little family at home. I had not realized how much I missed spending time with Bennet while our home was filled with guests. I will have to remember that if we are ever blessed with another child shortly before the holidays."

"Did you miss spending time only with Ben or perhaps your husband, as well?"

"You poor dear man, are you feeling neglected by your wife?" She teasingly asked as she slowly sauntered toward where her husband was sitting. "I would never wish to deprive you of my company, my dearest husband," Elizabeth said as she sat on Darcy's lap and caressed his face.

Darcy took her face into his hands and slowly brushed his thumbs across her cheeks. She lowered her head and began kissing her husband. "Mrs. Darcy, you have no idea what you do to me."

"Perhaps we should retire, and you can tell me all about it." At his wife's response, Darcy slowly rose without lowering Elizabeth to the floor. As they gazed lovingly into each other's eyes, they walked as one into their bed chamber and locked the door behind them.

LATER THAT NIGHT, AS ELIZABETH WAS ENJOYING HER

husband's embrace, she smiled at her happiness. Darcy quietly asked, "what are you thinking, my love?"

"I am thinking about how happy I am. We have a healthy son, I am well, and Georgiana is the perfect sister and aunt."

"What about me?"

"I thought I just showed you how much I love you, but if you need more proof…"

"No, I am just teasing you," He turned his head and kissed her hair. "I feel the same way. I enjoyed all our guests, but I am so happy to have you, Ben and Georgiana all to myself. I wish our new found peace could last forever, but, alas, it cannot."

Elizabeth quickly sat up and looked at her husband. "William, whatever do you mean? Is something wrong?"

"No, my dearest, nothing is wrong. You simply forgot that our sister is to make her debut into society in only a few months." She threw herself back into her pillows, covered her face and moaned as she continued to listen to her husband. "We must soon prepare to leave for London and plan for Georgiana's coming out. There is her presentation at Court, a ball at Darcy House to plan, and endless visits to the modistes. Then all the callers who will undoubtedly descend on Darcy House after she is presented to the *ton*."

She turned to her husband and said softly, "I suppose I am so happy we are finally alone that I put Georgiana's debut out of my head. I wish we could just stay here all the time, and never have to deal with any of the nonsense of the *ton*. And I am certain our sister would agree."

"You have no idea how much I wish for the same. However, are you not the same woman who is always reminding me that our sister is growing up and cannot always be part of our household?"

"If I said that, I was mistaken. I have decided that we will all stay here forever and never again go to Town and Georgiana will always be with us," Elizabeth teased. When she looked into her husband's eyes, she saw the pain he felt at the thought of Georgiana leaving them and one day starting a new life with her husband. Elizabeth knew Darcy would never deem any of their sister's prospective suitors as good enough, but she also knew he understood that there was no way to hold back the future.

"If you wish it, my dearest, then that is how it shall be." Darcy kissed his wife's hair, "at least for the next few weeks." He embraced his wife more tightly and added, "were you not about to show me how much you love me?" Elizabeth returned to her husband's embrace and there was no further discussion of their decamping for London for the remainder of the night.

PEACE AND QUIET REIGNED OVER PEMBERLEY FOR A FEW more days, although the three adult Darcys were all waiting until 'the discussion' would take place and change everything. They did not have to wait long, shortly after Twelfth Night, Georgiana entered the breakfast room holding a letter. "William, where is Lizzy? There is something we must all talk about."

"She is with Bennet in the nursery but should be here shortly. Is anything amiss?"

"No, but I have had another letter from Aunt Patricia, and she has so many questions about my presentation at Court and my coming out. I suppose it is time we begin planning the next few months." Elizabeth entered the room just as her sister finished speaking.

"Lizzy, I have been waiting for you. Aunt Patricia wrote me again yesterday about the upcoming Season and I did not want to respond to her without consulting you and William. I wish we could all stay here and enjoy Pemberley when the spring comes."

Darcy and Elizabeth looked at each other acknowledging the similarity of Georgiana's wishes to their own. "Elizabeth and I were just saying the same thing. We are all so happy here, why does everything have to change?"

"I feel terrible about having to upset everything, but we have put off answering Aunt Patricia's questions for too long. I believe we need to make some definite plans about our journey and my Ball and so many other things. When I was staying at Matlock Manor, we talked a great deal about my debut but in more general terms. I suppose now it is time to make some decisions."

Darcy looked first at his sister, then his wife. "When did our sister become an adult? She is ready to take charge of the entire enterprise. She will make certain everything we need is packed. She will ensure all of Bennet's needs are prepared as well and make all the arrangements for our journey. She shall decide when and where we will stop to rest and where to sleep. If we leave it to her, she will probably have her party at Darcy House planned as well!" They all laughed at William's loving tease.

"I love you both, and it matters not what the future brings, that will never change."

Elizabeth saw that Darcy had tears in his eyes as he listened to the young woman he had raised sound so grown up. "Well, Miss Darcy, I believe there is no time like the present. Shall we meet with Mrs. Reynolds and begin making our plans for our journey and all that awaits us in London?"

"That sounds like a wonderful idea. If you can wait a few minutes, I would like to have something to eat before we meet with Mrs. Reynolds. I was so afraid of what you would say this morning that I hardly ate any dinner last night. Thank you for understanding and helping me through the next stressful months of our lives."

LATER THAT MORNING, MRS. ANNESLEY WAS SHOWN into Darcy's study. "Thank you for seeing me, sir."

"Are you well, Mrs. Annesley? You know we consider you to be part of our family. If there is anything you require, you need only ask."

"That is why I have asked to see you privately, Mr. Darcy. My daughter was married shortly before I became Miss Georgiana's companion. She is going to give birth to her first child in March and asked if I could come and stay with her and her husband in Bath. Now that you and Mrs. Darcy have your own family and Georgiana is so much better than she was when I met her, I think the time for her needing my services has passed. I thought I would discuss it with you before I spoke to your sister about it."

"I suppose you are correct when saying Georgiana no longer requires a companion and we would never attempt to prevent you from being with your daughter at such an important time." Darcy paused, "would you like me to speak to my sister about it?"

"Yes, I would appreciate you telling her first. I will speak to her afterward and would like to stay on until the family returns to London. I will be sorry to miss Georgiana's debut, but my daughter needs me more."

"Leave it to me, Mrs. Annesley. I can never thank you enough for everything you have done for my sister and our family."

"It has been my pleasure, sir, and I will miss you all when I leave your home."

~

AT BIRCHWOOD MANOR, CHARLES ROSE FROM THE breakfast table and kissed his wife before leaving the room. A few minutes later, as Jane rose to leave, Caroline asked, "do you have a few minutes this morning to talk?"

"Of course, I hope you are enjoying your stay. Is anything wrong?"

"I am enjoying my stay in Derbyshire more than I ever dreamed possible. I need some advice and I believe you are the one person I can trust to tell me the truth."

"How can I help you?"

"I believe I have fallen in love and I do not know how to proceed from here."

"Who, may I ask, is the object of your affection? I have an idea, but I would rather hear it from you."

"Peter Carter, the vicar at Kympton. We have had several conversations and we danced at the Harvest Ball and Boxing Day and at the Twelfth Night party. We talked about so many things when we sat next to each other at Christmas dinner. I am certain you would never believe that I could consider a man without great wealth or a title, but there it is. I think I love him. When I see him, my heart begins to pound, and my knees are weak. Jane, what am I to do? Please, tell me the truth."

"There is not much I can say. I am happy you have chosen to love someone based on their character and not on the trappings of the *ton*. You have not told me how Mr. Carter feels about you."

"I am not sure. He seeks me out whenever our paths cross and he told me at the Christmas dinner that he was happy I was staying in Derbyshire. How can I be sure of his feelings? If he does not care for me, I do not know what I shall do. I think about him all the time and I dream of him at night. Jane, please tell me what to do."

"If Mr. Carter feels the same affection for you, you will soon know it." Before she could say any more, a footman knocked and entered the room.

"Pardon me, madam, but you have a caller."

"Did they leave their card, Jenkins?"

"Yes, it is a Mr. Carter, ma'am."

Jane looked at Caroline and smiled. "Please show Mr. Carter into the drawing room and ask Mrs. Wilson for some tea." The footman bowed to Jane and exited the room.

"Can it be true? Has he really come to Birchwood to see me? I do not know what to say or how to act; this is an entirely new experience for me."

"You will be fine, Caroline. Try to keep calm and respond politely to anything Mr. Carter asks. Now, let us go. We do not wish to keep your caller waiting, do we?"

"No, we do not. Thank you for your advice. You are a wonderful sister; you are much kinder to me than I deserve."

"Nonsense, Caroline, you deserve every happiness. Now let us go!" Both sisters were smiling as they entered the drawing room and greeted Mr. Carter.

A FEW DAYS AFTER THE DECISION TO LEAVE PEMBERLEY was made, Darcy asked his sister to join him in his study after breakfast. "Mrs. Annesley has a married daughter who lives in Bath. Her daughter has asked her mother to come and live with her family and help her with the new baby. I know we shall all miss her but I believe your need for a companion has long passed. How do you feel about it, Georgie?"

"She told me her daughter, Margaret, was increasing. I can certainly understand her desire to be with her. I will miss her but I do not wish to keep her from being with her own family. When does she plan to leave for Bath?"

"Shortly before we leave for London, I will send her in one of our carriages and make all the arrangements for her journey. It is time she moved on to her new responsibilities as a grandmother."

"I suppose this is the first of the many changes in my life over the next few months."

"All will be well, little one. All will be well." Darcy embraced his sister and did not see the tears that filled her eyes.

****

Over the following weeks, Elizabeth and Mrs. Reynolds reviewed the packing list over and over again and the Darcys were finally prepared for their removal to Darcy House. Shortly before their departure, they all were sad when Mrs. Annesley left for Bath. Darcy repeatedly expressed his thanks for her coming into his sister's life and helping her get passed the ordeal of Ramsgate. Elizabeth and Georgiana hugged Mrs. Annesley and everyone promised to write. The Darcys stood together on the front steps and watched until the carriage conveying her to Bath was out of sight.

Their journey to London was longer than usual; they were delayed at times due to the weather and at other times due to the demands of traveling with an infant. Eventually, everyone had arrived safely at Darcy House and was quickly settled in. Mrs. Winters, their housekeeper, was thrilled to have a baby in the house once again. She and all the young maids were taken with young master Bennet, who never had to wait very long for someone to pick him up and cuddle with him.

Before they left Derbyshire, Georgiana and Elizabeth were in frequent correspondence with Lady Matlock regarding the exciting events of the next few months. After arriving in Town, Darcy sat back and watched Georgiana and Elizabeth's efforts to accomplish everything that needed to be done without his interference. He observed that by the time they all sat down to dinner, his two favorite women looked so tired that he feared they might fall asleep during their meal. After one such evening, Darcy spoke to his wife as they prepared for bed. "You cannot keep up this pace, my love. You look so tired and I fear for your health as well as my sister's. I know you want everything to be perfect for her but I also know that you wish to spend more time with Bennet. You and I have not had a real conversation since arriving in Town."

"I know," Elizabeth said while stifling a yawn, "it just seems that there is so much more to be done. I have been trying to wake up early enough to spend time with Ben before starting my day. Every time Georgiana and I get something accomplished, several more things are urgently in need of our attention. Aunt Patricia has been wonderful; thank heaven she will present Georgiana at Court and eliminate any need for my participation. She loves our sister so much and wants everything to be perfect for her debut in three weeks."

"I appreciate everything you are doing to make our sister feel special. Now, get into bed, wife!"

"I am perfectly happy to obey you, my husband." Elizabeth forced a tired smile and followed William into bed. He extended his arm and she entered his embrace; within a moment he knew she was already asleep. He smiled to himself as he happily thought that, in a few short weeks, this would all be behind them.

CHAPTER 13

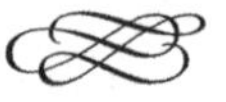

LONDON

Lord and Lady Matlock arrived in Town shortly after their holiday stay at Pemberley. Lady Matlock, Elizabeth and Georgiana were frequent correspondents before they were reunited in London. As the mother of two boys, Patricia Matlock doted on her niece as she would her own daughter. In early February, Richard joined his parents and was eager to participate in the most important event of Georgiana's first Season.

Upon her youngest son's return to Town, Lady Matlock spoke to her husband of her renewed determination to find a wife for Richard. One morning shortly after he arrived in London, Richard and his parents were seated together at the breakfast table. His mother began the same conversation she and her son had often struggled through in the past. "Richard, my dear boy, it is time for you to find a wife. You have been all alone as the master of

Rosings for long enough. I know any number of beautiful young women who would be more than happy to marry you and become the mistress of such a beautiful estate. I have set up some small dinner parties and you can see how well you get along with the daughters of some of our friends. You will also be able to meet any number of eligible women during the best events of the Season."

"Thank you, Mama, but I believe I am quite capable of finding a wife on my own. And, I do not plan to remain in London for more than a few days after Georgiana's Ball. There is much for me to do before the spring plantings."

"Hugh, tell your son how important it is that he find a wife. When you were in His Majesty's Army, we could understand your reluctance to marry and subject your poor wife to long periods without her husband by her side. Now, there is no excuse not to wed. Leave it to me, I will take care of everything!"

"Richard, I must agree with your mother. You are not getting any younger and you certainly have the wealth to support a family. It will not hurt you to attend a few dinner parties and you may be surprised; there may be someone who strikes your fancy."

"Please, father, not you too?"

"We will let you know when your presence is required at dinner. I heard that Lady Howard is in

London for the Season. She is quite lovely and is finally finished mourning that awful Lord Howard. I enjoyed being in her company during the festivities at Pemberley, although she seemed very quiet. Perhaps she can be our guest of honor at one of our dinners."

"I can see that you will not take 'no' for an answer, but I will only attend three events before returning to Kent and Georgiana's Ball is one of them. As for Lady Howard, I would ask that you not involve her in your scheming. I am going to my club and wish you both a good day," Richard rose and quickly left the family dining room.

"Patricia, did you see his reaction when you mentioned Lady Howard? Perhaps there is some interest there despite his words of protest."

"Time will tell, my husband. Now, I must start making a list of potential women to invite to dinner," Lady Matlock rose and kissed her husband's cheek before walking toward her private study.

The following morning the trio was once again at the breakfast table. "I visited my club yesterday and all anyone could talk about was how happy they were that the fog has finally lifted. Was it really as bad as all that?"

"Indeed, it was probably worse than you heard and thankfully, it ended shortly after we arrived in London. According to some of our friends, at its worst, the fog was so thick that people in the street were walking into walls and carriages were crashing into each other. We heard it was like nothing anyone had ever seen before and I pray it never returns."

"I am glad that you were not affected by the fog when you arrived. I wish you both a good day," he rose and bowed to his parents before exiting the house.

RICHARD THOUGHT ABOUT LADY EMILY DAY AND NIGHT, but he was afraid that if he saw her again and seemed too eager to be near her, she would reject his attention. He learned the Darcys had arrived in Town and when he left Matlock House that morning, he went to speak with the Darcys about his feelings.

He was quickly admitted by the footman and shown into Darcy's unoccupied study. A few minutes later he was joined by both his cousins. "Richard, what a wonderful surprise! We are so happy to see you. Georgiana is with her music teacher but she will join us shortly. How are you, cousin?"

"I am quite well, Lizzy, I hope you were not affected by the fog. My parents told me how terrible it was."

"Happily, we arrived in London when the fog was almost gone. What brings you here today, Richard?"

"I have several reasons for my visit; I wanted to welcome you to London, and I am looking forward to seeing Georgiana. I also came here to talk to you both about a very private matter." Darcy and Elizabeth exchanged puzzled looks before he said, "you know you can tell us anything and we will never betray your confidence."

"I know I can trust you both but there is not much mystery as to what I wish to talk to you about. I am madly in love with Lady Emily Howard and have no idea how to win her affection."

"Are you sure that she does not already feel affection for you?"

"She has always been very polite but, I have seen no signs of affection when we are together."

"How can we help you? We will do anything we can to help you win Lady Emily's heart."

"I thank you, Darcy, but I have no idea where to begin."

"William and I fell in love while we were walking and talking about anything that popped into our heads. I am confident that when Lady Emily spends enough time with you, she will be unable to resist your charms."

"Elizabeth is correct, you must spend time together and really get to know each other. Your acquaintance has not been of long duration and for most of that time she was still mourning her husband."

"Mama is determined to find a wife for me. She is planning some small dinner parties, so I can meet and get to know some of the *ton's* finest. She also mentioned that she knew Lady Emily was here for the Season, but I asked her not to throw us together in such an intimate setting."

"Would you like us to invite Lady Emily to Georgiana's Ball? I have heard that she is staying with her parents and it would not be a problem to include all of them."

"I thank you, but I want to focus all my attention that night on Georgiana. If I am distracted by Lady Emily's presence, I fear I may be tempted to pay our beautiful girl less attention than she deserves."

They spoke about several other scenarios where Richard and Lady Emily might get to know each other, and Elizabeth summed it all up. "If you really love Lady Emily, you must spend as much time as possible together. When the right moment presents itself, tell her how you feel. It is important to let her understand your feelings and why you wish to marry her. You must make it very clear how very different your marriage would be from the nightmare she experienced with Lord Howard."

Richard was quiet while he attempted to formulate a plan to win the heart and hand of Lady Emily. "I thank you both; you have given me much to ponder. I am so grateful to have you as cousins but equally grateful to have you as friends. I believe I will take a long walk and gather my thoughts; I do have some experience with tactics and strategy. I need to determine how to best apply those skills to wooing the woman of my dreams. Tell Georgiana I will return tomorrow to see her."

"Richard, we have every confidence that you will be successful in winning her heart. If there is anything we can do, please do not hesitate to ask." Richard bowed and kissed Elizabeth's hand before leaving Darcy House.

WHEN RICHARD RETURNED HOME AFTER HIS TALK WITH the Darcys, Lady Matlock informed her son that she was having a dinner party the following night. She told him that there would be three outstanding young women in attendance and asked him to be on his best behavior. "Madam, I am not a child you must tell how to behave. I am a grown man with a mind of my own."

"I am very aware of that fact, but I think you need to be more open to new ideas and new people."

"I will try my best to be an obedient son tomorrow night."

"I also accepted an invitation on your behalf to attend Lord and Lady Townsend's Ball which is shortly after Georgiana's debut. You know that Lady Townsend and I have been friends since we were in school. I believe the Darcys are also planning to attend. My dear son, attending a private ball is not the end of the world and if you so desire, you can always join your cousin and stand against the wall of the ballroom with a scowl on your face. Although, I must say, being married to Elizabeth has helped Darcy become a more sociable person."

"I will attend the dinner party tomorrow night and the party at the Townsend's, but I will not be forced to attend any other events. I love you, Mama, but I am fully capable of finding myself a wife. Good day, my lady."

~

RICHARD ENTERED THE DRAWING ROOM AT MATLOCK House and noticed that all of the dinner guests had already arrived. *These people must be desperate to find husbands for their daughters if they arrive before the appointed time on their invitations.* Lady Matlock noticed Richard's entrance and was quickly by his side. She took his arm and walked him around the room and introduced him to all their guests. Shortly after the introductions were made, a footman entered the room to announce that dinner was served.

One of the *outstanding* young women he had just met was quickly at his side. She placed her hand on his arm and he forced a smile as he escorted Lady Amelia Stafford into dinner. Once they entered the dining room, Richard noted where he and Lady Amelia were seated. *I see that it was no coincidence that*

I escorted her; I am also seated next to Lady Amelia. My mother and her matchmaking! She must think Lady Amelia is the top choice of the potential wife candidates tonight!

As soon as she and Richard were seated, Lady Amelia began the conversation. "Mr. Fitzwilliam, your mother was telling me about your bravery and leadership while you were serving in His Majesty's Army. Do you miss the army? Do you enjoy being a gentleman farmer? I imagine there is not much your two vocations have in common. I do like a man in uniform; all the ribbons and medals are so colorful. And the gold buttons, my goodness, they take my breath away." *I am utterly delighted Mama seated me next to this woman. She does not seem to come up for air and it leaves me free to enjoy my dinner without having to say a word.* The remainder of the evening was much the same, but Richard was true to his promise of listening and smiling politely to the very talkative and inquisitive Lady Amelia.

When all their guests had left for the night, Lady Matlock took Richard's arm as they walked back to the drawing room. "You seemed to have enjoyed your time with your dinner companion; I seated her next to you because I thought you two would suit more than the other ladies I invited. Do you think there is any future for you and Amelia?"

"Mama, Lady Amelia is a magpie; she did not stop talking for the entire meal. She asked me question after question but never stop speaking long enough to allow me to answer. I think her questions were rehearsed and she was so unsure of herself, she just kept asking them. I am sorry to disappoint you, my lady, but I will not be calling on Lady Amelia tomorrow or any other day. I thank you for the effort, but I am quite tired and bid you goodnight." Richard kissed his mother's cheek and left the room.

DARCY, ELIZABETH AND GEORGIANA EXCHANGED reassuring smiles as they waited by the front door for the Matlock carriage to arrive. Georgiana looked beautiful, but her Court dress was the most elaborate, over-enhanced garment any of them had ever seen. Elizabeth knew she would never feel comfortable wearing the feather covered headpiece that Lady Matlock had chosen for her sister. She said a silent prayer of thanks that Aunt Patricia was taking her sister to be presented at Court; sparing her from the additional ordeal of having to wear a dress and headpiece similar to Georgiana's.

Elizabeth had been presented at Court several years prior and she was dressed much more simply. The economic status of her family was far below that of the young woman standing anxiously beside her. Georgiana was so nervous before Lady Matlock arrived, that she refused to eat anything in fear she would be sick. When the Matlock carriage finally appeared, Darcy and Elizabeth walked outside with their sister to welcome Lady Matlock. They kissed their sister for luck and Elizabeth discreetly handed Lady Matlock a napkin containing some biscuits for Georgiana to eat on their return.

When it was time for them to enter the Court, her Aunt Patricia said, "Just remember one thing, never turn your back on royalty. Curtsy once when you enter the room, once when you are standing before their Highnesses and once more as we exit." Georgiana felt she might faint at any moment, but she frequently looked at her aunt for guidance and got through her presentation without a mistake. Upon entering the Matlock carriage for their return to Darcy House, Georgiana smiled and said, "Aunt Patricia, I cannot thank you enough for today and all you did to prepare me. I am so relieved it is over; now I feel I could eat an entire roast lamb!"

The two women laughed, and Lady Matlock remembered the napkin Elizabeth handed her when they entered the carriage. "I believe Elizabeth was thoughtful enough to anticipate your hunger and sent these along."

She gave her niece the napkin and when Georgiana saw her favorite biscuits, she smiled brightly and said, "Lizzy is the best sister I could ever ask for. She and William are so happy, and it is so easy to see their love. I hope that one day I will meet someone who will make me as happy as William makes Lizzy."

"Elizabeth is a remarkable woman and I am so pleased that theirs is a true love match. I have no doubt that when the right man comes along, you will know it. Getting your brother to agree to granting your suitor a courtship or betrothal is another matter." Lady Matlock smiled and looked out the carriage window for a moment. When she looked back at her niece, Georgiana was busily devouring the sweet treats that her thoughtful sister had sent along.

CHAPTER 14

Every day after her presentation to the Court, Georgiana and Elizabeth worked with Mrs. Winters, and Lady Matlock making sure that the night of Georgiana's Ball would be perfect. There were frequent visits to the modiste, shoemakers and many other vendors to complete the list of Georgiana's needs.

Several days before the Ball, Elizabeth received two express letters from her sisters Jane and Catherine. Jane told her that she and Charles would not be able to come to London for Georgiana's debut as planned. Maddie had a cold which had gotten worse and the doctor thought traveling to London would be detrimental to her condition. Elizabeth knew the Bingleys would not think of leaving their sick child for so long. Elizabeth also received a letter from her sister, Catherine, with the happy news was that she had given birth to a healthy baby girl named Jane Elizabeth. She was feeling well and was anticipating the Darcys' return to Derbyshire, so they could meet their new niece. They sent their regrets and best wishes to the debutante.

That evening while preparing for bed, Elizabeth told her husband about the news she had received from her family "I do not think we ever expected Catherine and David to accept our invitation so soon after Catherine giving birth. I am disappointed that Jane and Charles will be unable to join us, but I know we would do the same. Bennet has never been sick, but I know we would never think of leaving him if he was not well."

"Of course, you are correct and we will see the Bingleys as soon as we return to Pemberley. Georgiana is very fond of Jane and Charles and I know they will be missed, but she will understand their reasons for remaining at home."

"We are going to the modiste in the morning for our final fittings. She looks so lovely in her gown; when we were at the modiste last week, I nearly cried when I saw her looking so elegant and grown up. The dress is so beautiful and I believe she feels more confident when she wears it. I want to be completely honest with you, we both heard some cutting remarks while we were there. Some of London's high society matrons were talking about our marriage and the disparity of our stations in the *ton*. I knew Georgiana was upset by what she heard but I assured her that no matter what others say, you and I have a marriage built on love, trust and respect. I believe that Georgiana will choose very carefully when the time comes."

"Why did you not tell me that some horrid old cows were rude to you? I will make sure they never set foot in this house or Matlock House ever again. Who were they?"

"I did not know the women and their remarks had no effect on me. Please do not be distressed by anything those 'horrid old cows' said about me. We love each other and nothing anyone says can ever change that. Now, it is time for bed; I have an early appointment with the modiste."

As they got into bed, Darcy embraced his wife and kissed her hair. "You never cease to amaze me, my dearest. You are so strong and so true to yourself; I am so happy I had the good sense to marry you."

"*You* had the good sense, what about *my* good sense?" Their lips met for a moment and they were both smiling as they fell asleep in each other's arms.

~

THE DAY OF GEORGIANA'S BALL FINALLY ARRIVED. LADY Matlock sent several of her servants to supplement the staff of Darcy House and they all worked hard to make the house sparkle and shine. The flower arrangements were the most beautiful Elizabeth had ever seen and she made one last visit to the kitchen before preparing for the evening. She knew that the food would be delicious if their aromas were any indication. Lady Matlock had used her influence and convinced the most sought-after musicians to play for her niece's introduction into London's highest social circle.

At last, Hannah had finished helping her dress, styling her hair and closing the clasp on the beautiful pearl necklace Darcy had given his wife for her birthday. Elizabeth descended the stairs of Darcy House and saw her husband waiting for her near the front door. He looked up at her with adoration in his eyes and she smiled as she slowly walked toward her husband. She wore a beautiful cream-colored dress with a gold lace overlay; there were cream colored roses placed among her curls and decorating her satin slippers. She knew she had never looked better.

Darcy kissed her gloved hand and said quietly, "Elizabeth, you look like a goddess, but I am afraid you must go back upstairs and change your dress."

"Change my dress? You do not like it?" Elizabeth asked in a panicked voice and on the verge of tears.

"No, my love, you look stunning, but I wish you would change your dress for two reasons."

"I am waiting, Mr. Darcy." she relaxed and tapped

her toes in mock impatience now that she knew her husband was teasing her.

"If you wear that dress, I cannot guarantee that I will not ravish you in the middle of the ballroom before the night is over. Secondly, you look so beautiful that I must remind you that Georgiana must be the center of attention tonight."

Before she could tease her husband in return, Mrs. Winters joined them in the front entry hall. They all looked up to see Georgiana coming slowly down the stairs. She looked like an angel; her beautiful blonde hair was pinned up in a sophisticated style and there were small pearls placed throughout her curls. Her dress was a very pale pink and the white lace overlay was also decorated with pearls. As she moved toward them, Elizabeth and Darcy knew they were about to enter a new phase of their lives.

"Georgie, you look so beautiful, what has happened to my silly little sister? You know the girl who only wanted to ride her pony and make mud pies?"

"Do you really like my dress? Elizabeth and Aunt Patricia helped me choose it. Is it too much with all the pearls?"

"You are a beautiful young woman and there is not one thing I would change about you or the way you look tonight."

"Thank you, William, I am so glad you like my dress."

"Georgie, I love everything about you every day. Tonight, you look extraordinarily beautiful."

Mrs. Winters approached the trio. "Excuse me sir, madam, I believe I hear a carriage outside. Your guests are beginning to arrive and you should form the receiving line before anyone enters. Everything is ready in the ballroom and the musicians are warming up. If I may say so, Mrs. Darcy and Miss Georgiana look absolutely beautiful."

"Thank you, Mrs. Winters, we will line up in a moment. I think we are all relishing the quiet while it lasts," Darcy responded. He turned away from his wife and sister, moved closer to the housekeeper and said quietly, "Does everyone know what actions to take if a certain uninvited guest arrives?"

"Yes sir, everyone is ready to act, if necessary."

"William, we should follow Mrs. Winters' advice; I can also hear our guests beginning to arrive." Her husband nodded and took both women by the arm and led them to the spot where they would be greeting their guests. Darcy was first, then Elizabeth and finally, Georgiana Darcy making her debut in London society. Elizabeth looked at Darcy with a question in her eyes.

"I will tell you all about it later; it is nothing to be

worried about. Let me just say, no one will do anything to spoil Georgiana's special night." Elizabeth smiled and was determined to forget what she had just heard and enjoy the evening.

Georgiana was relieved when the Fitzwilliams were among the first to arrive. Her aunt and uncle were very dear to her and she loved Richard as a brother. She relied on their familiar faces to maintain her composure and boost her confidence.

Despite her misgivings, Georgiana was beautiful and poised as she greeted her guests at the Ball. The temperature outside was well below freezing but nothing could prevent London's finest from witnessing the debut of a young woman from one of the wealthiest families in England.

DARCY DANCED THE FIRST DANCE WITH HIS SISTER AND had never been prouder of the young woman on his arm. While she danced the second set with her cousin, she could sense everyone's eyes were still on her. She began to feel anxious about what would happen when her set with Richard ended. She hoped that other men would ask her to dance; no debutante wished to stand against the wall watching other young women enjoying the dancing at *her* Ball.

When the second set ended, Georgiana need not have worried, she was besieged by a long line of young men for a place on her dance card. By the time the party was over, she had danced every dance. She ate supper with a large crowd of young men all vying for an opportunity to sit beside her or bring her something to eat and drink. She danced the supper set with a young man named David Arlington and he escorted her into the meal. "May I prepare a plate for you, Miss Darcy?"

"Thank you, that would be most kind of you." When he returned to the table, David Arlington was carrying two plates of roast chicken, potatoes and vegetables. "I hope you approve of my selections?"

"Thank you, sir, you have chosen all of my favorites," she smiled as she spoke to her new acquaintance.

When their last guests had departed early the next morning, Elizabeth, Darcy and Georgiana were all exhausted. "How are you feeling, little one? You have had quite an eventful night! I believe you danced every dance."

"I am so happy this night is behind me. I did enjoy dancing all night, but I liked some dances more than others." Before she could explain her comments, she added, "Lizzy, please allow me to thank you again for all your help. I am so happy you are my sister and I know I can always rely on you and William for support. Pray excuse me, I am dreadfully tired. I will see you both in the morning, or I should say, later this morning." Georgiana embraced her sister before turning into her brother's arms.

"Good night, little one. We are very proud of you."

Before Elizabeth and Darcy followed Georgiana up the stairs, Mrs. Winters approached them, "Mr. Darcy, may I have a moment of your time?"

"Certainly." Darcy turned to his wife, "I will join you upstairs in a moment."

"Good night Mrs. Winters and thank you for all your help. Miss Darcy's party was a huge success and we are all very grateful. So many of the guests commented on all the delicious food; particularly the puddings and cakes that were served for dessert."

"I am happy you are pleased, madam, good night."

Darcy followed his housekeeper into the drawing room, "what happened?"

"You were right to warn the staff, sir. Lady Catherine tried to push her way into the party. Happily, when she attempted to enter, the music was very loud and no one at the party could hear her."

"What did she say? Tell me everything."

"What did she not say? She began by criticizing the butler, the footmen and me. When she tried to move toward the ballroom, she raised her cane to strike one of the footmen who had blocked her path and she was physically restrained, as you asked. She began screaming about you and Mrs. Darcy and how you have ruined Miss Darcy's life by marrying…"

"Go on, I need to hear everything."

"Needless to say, Lady Catherine is most displeased with Mrs. Darcy. That was all she said before Watkins and Jackson lifted her and carried her down the front steps and put her back in her carriage."

"Thank you, Mrs. Winters. I appreciate your honesty. I am very pleased that everyone carried out my directions. If it is at all possible, I would appreciate your discretion in this matter. I will tell Mrs. Darcy what happened tonight but I see no reason for my sister to find out."

"I have already spoken to the staff about keeping what they saw here tonight to themselves."

"Good night, Mrs. Winters and thank you again."

"Good night, sir." The housekeeper walked back toward the servants' quarters as Darcy climbed the stairs shaking his head. He could not believe that his aunt would dare to enter a party to which she had not been invited. He knew he had to tell Elizabeth, but the news could wait until they were well rested.

AFTER HIS CONVERSATION WITH THE HOUSEKEEPER, HE went upstairs and prepared for bed. He joined his wife in her chambers, and they sat beside each other on the settee.

"Elizabeth, you have amazed me once again. You planned the most wonderful night for Georgiana as if you had done it many times before. Thank you, my love. Georgiana will never forget how special her debut was."

"I love her as I love my other sisters. There is nothing I would not do for her and Aunt Patricia's help was invaluable. Why did Mrs. Winters wish to speak to you after the party?"

"I was going to tell you after we had a good night's sleep, but I should have realized that you always know when I am trying to keep something from you." Darcy paused and took his wife's hand. "I was afraid that my Aunt Catherine would try to barge in and ruin Georgiana's big night. I told Mrs. Winters to inform the footmen that if she did try to intrude, she should be unceremoniously carried out of the house. Mrs. Winters told me that my aunt tried to push her way in and tried to strike some of our staff with her cane when they prevented her from doing so. Several of the footmen were needed to pick her up and put her back in her carriage. All is well, and Georgiana will never know of the disturbance."

She caressed her husband's cheek. "You think of everything, my love. Thank you for keeping us all safe and not allowing anyone or anything to spoil our sister's party. Did Lady Catherine say anything when she barged in?"

"Nothing we have not heard before. She came in spewing her vitriol and she would not leave on her own accord. I will speak to my Uncle Hugh tomorrow. There is something significantly wrong with my aunt and we must take steps to prevent her from saying or doing anything that could injure our family."

"I take it to mean that your aunt said some very unflattering words about me. Am I correct?"

"What my aunt does or does not say should be of no concern to you, my love. They are the ravings of a vicious, bitter woman who has lost control of her senses." Darcy kissed his wife's hand, "are you happy now that you know everything?"

Elizabeth nodded, "I appreciate you telling me the truth." She paused, "I feel sorry for your aunt."

"Sorry?" Darcy asked incredulously. "Whatever for?"

"We have so much love and happiness in our lives and she has gone about destroying everything good in hers. I know she is unkind, but I still feel sorry for her."

"That is because you are a kind, forgiving woman. You are everything my aunt is not. Did you enjoy yourself tonight?"

"Yes, I was very happy everything turned out so well. I am curious about Georgiana's last comment; she said she enjoyed some dances more than others. Do you think she already has feelings for one of the young men on her dance card?"

"Please, Elizabeth, I cannot fall asleep with that thought on my mind."

"Well, perhaps I can clear your mind by offering you something better to think about," Elizabeth teased as she continued to caress her husband's face.

"Did I tell you how much I love you, Mrs. Darcy?"

"Mr. Darcy, your secret is safe with me."

CHAPTER 15

Darcy House was very quiet the following morning as all the party goers slept late. By the time three very tired people descended the stairs, it was almost midday. They knew that many of the young men who lined up to dance with Georgiana would also call upon her today. They expected to receive the first callers by the early afternoon and were not disappointed. One young man after another, presented their cards at the door. When they were admitted to the drawing room, they saw Georgiana surrounded by other eager young men.

Darcy was exhausted and had a fierce scowl on his face. He was in no mood to entertain these young men who dared to show an interest in his sister. Elizabeth attempted to ease his obvious disapproval of every young man who dared to call on the beautiful Georgiana Darcy. She frequently touched his arm, reminding him that no matter how he felt about the situation, these gentlemen were their guests.

Elizabeth knew her husband was upset and planned to speak to him as soon as their guests departed. Later that afternoon, Elizabeth stood outside her husband's study and could hear him pacing and mumbling under his breath. Her knock was answered with a brusque, "Enter!"

She walked into the room and went to her husband and embraced him. "What was that for?"

"Do I need a reason to embrace the man I love?"

"I know you are here to tell me something and I would appreciate it if you would just come out with it," he said impatiently.

"I can easily see how watching Georgiana entertain her callers gives you pain. William, at some point in the next year or two or three, Georgiana will fall in love with someone wonderful. There is no point in pacing and scowling every day until that day comes. When she is ready, we will not be able to stop her from wanting to marry. When we fell in love, no one or nothing could stop our feelings. I am not happy about her leaving us one day, but we must be realistic."

"I know what you are saying is the truth, I just do not wish her to be taken in by some rake or fortune hunter."

"I think Georgiana will know who loves her, not her thirty-thousand-pound dowry. She learned a valuable lesson in Ramsgate and is growing up. We must let her know just how much we trust her and value her feelings. You told me you were going to see Lord Matlock today to discuss your aunt's behavior."

"That is a good idea. It is past time to do something about her. Her vitriol is hurting the entire family."

"I will see you later for dinner."

"Thank you for coming in here and trying to make me feel better. Your kindness never ceases to amaze me."

"You are very easy to be kind to. I have already sent her a note, but if you see Aunt Patricia, please thank her again for everything she did. I could not have planned such a successful party without her." Darcy kissed his wife and prepared to leave the house.

Despite the cold, Darcy decided to walk the short distance to Matlock House and he was soon seated in his uncle's study. "I am so glad to see you! Georgiana's party was well done. My little niece looked so lovely, as did your beautiful wife."

"Thank you, uncle. Georgiana and Elizabeth are very grateful for Aunt Patricia's help. Last night's party is actually why I am here."

"Did something happen that I was not aware of?"

"Pray allow me to start at the beginning. We invited Aunt Catherine to our wedding and her reply was a thick letter accusing me of causing Anne's death and disgracing the family name by marrying Elizabeth. She failed to acknowledge that Anne had already passed away by the time I recovered enough to return to England. I only read the first page of her cruel accusations and then I threw it in the fire. I sent my aunt an announcement of Ben's birth which she returned to me unopened."

"So far, it sounds like typical Catherine behavior. If you do not follow her commands, she becomes very angry. There must be something else."

"When I received the note unopened, I made peace with the idea of never seeing or hearing from my aunt again. However, knowing her as I do, when we came to London, I put some security measures in place. I instructed my household staff that if Lady Catherine tried to enter my home uninvited, they were to physically carry her out."

"Darcy, your own aunt! My sister!"

"My fear was that she would try to disrupt and ruin Georgiana's party. She must have known that most of the *ton* was invited and would be at Darcy House last night. Before any guests arrived, Mrs. Winters assured me that everyone knew what to do. As you are aware, the party was a huge success from start to finish.

"When the final guests departed, Elizabeth and Georgiana went up to bed. Mrs. Winters told me then that Lady Catherine arrived when the party was well under way. She pushed her way into the house and began spouting her usual venom. She was screaming that my marrying Elizabeth would ruin Georgiana's chances to make a good match. Thankfully when she entered, she was drowned out by the music in the ballroom. Following my orders, several of my footmen picked her up despite her trying to strike them with her cane, carried her outside, and put her back into her carriage. Uncle, I come here today looking for some help. I believe Aunt Catherine has lost her mind and is obsessed with destroying my family. You understand that I will do everything necessary to protect the people I love."

Lord Matlock shook his head in disbelief. "I did not realize how serious this situation has become. What can be done? Must she be sent to Bedlam? My own sister, treating Anne's children so badly. What can we do?"

"Uncle, you are the head of our family and I trust you will do whatever it takes to insure the safety and well-being of all of us."

"Let me think about this for a few days. I will go to see Catherine myself and confront her with the information you have shared with me today."

"Be prepared to hear insults and condemnation as you have never heard before. She will start by condemning Richard for throwing her out of Rosings. She neglects to remember that he offered her the dower house which she refused."

"When I do see my sister, I believe I will bring some of our more muscular footmen with me. I do not want to seem vulnerable to anything she may say or do to me. Thank you for coming today. I am relieved that Catherine failed to achieve her goal last night."

"Thank you, Uncle Hugh. I look forward to hearing about the results of your meeting. Farewell until then."

AFTER SEVERAL MORE DAYS OF CALLERS, GEORGIANA asked Elizabeth if they might speak privately in her sitting room. As soon as they were seated, her sister began the conversation. "So many of the men I danced with at my party have continued to call on me."

"Yes, and for the most part, I thought they were all quite nice. Has anyone special come to call on you? Is there someone you would like to know better?"

"Lizzy, how did you know that you were in love with my brother?"

"Before I try to answer your question, I would like to remind you of one thing. You are very young and there is no reason to rush into marriage. You may not find someone you wish to marry this year or next year or the year after that. When you meet the right man, you will know it.

"How did I know I loved William? I fell in love with him while we were together in Hertfordshire. We walked together almost every day and we talked about everything; books, music, our love of nature and so many other things. As I got to know him better, I began to think about him more and more every day and I looked forward to seeing him whenever I could. On the days we could not be together, we were both in foul moods.

"We were separated for a long time while he was in Scotland recovering and I did not know he was alive. When Richard came to Longbourn to tell me the bad news, he gave me William's signet ring. I put it on a chain and wore it close to my heart where no one could see it. I mourned him for many, many months and eventually I came to realize that somehow I had to move on with my life. I had worn his ring for a year; one morning I woke up and I knew it was time to put it in my jewelry box.

"I allowed myself to grow fond of someone else when we thought…well, you know what we thought. I did enjoy spending time with David Brooks but in my heart, I did not feel for him what I felt for William. I was living at Birchwood and I was very sad and lonely; every day I saw how happy Jane and Charles were. I suppose I just wanted to have someone care about me the way Charles cared about Jane. I accepted Lord Winthrope's proposal in the hope that I would eventually come to love him.

"When your brother came back into my life, I knew I could never marry anyone else but him. Whenever I thought about the future, I could not see myself with anyone but William. I told Brooks that I could not marry him and he took the news better than I expected. Perhaps he did not love me as much as I thought. When he was introduced to my sister, Catherine, at the Bingley's Summer Ball, they felt an instant attraction which has only grown stronger every day since the day they met."

"Why did you fall in love with William? What did my brother do that made you love him?"

"Everyone is different, but I think there are certain feelings you experience when the potential for love is there. One of the things I liked most about your brother is that he listened to me. He thought about what I said and treated me as an intellectual equal. We also laughed a lot about some of the silliest things. Did we always agree? No, but we respected each other's opinions."

"I hope that someday I can love someone as you love William."

"I am certain you will. You will know when you meet

the right man. Do you think you have met anyone special?"

"Did you meet David Arlington? I danced the supper set with him at my party and he escorted me into the dining room. He even asked me for a second set, but my dance card was already full. He was very nice, and we seemed to have many things to talk about, but he has not come to call on me. I suppose he was not really interested in getting to know me better."

So, there is someone special. I knew she would not have made that statement about enjoying some dances more than others if there was not someone she wanted to spend more time with. "It may have been necessary for Mr. Arlington to attend to some pressing matters of business or perhaps he had to go out of town before he could pay a call. Do not fret, my sweet sister, if you are meant to be together, you will see each other again.

At his wife's suggestion, Darcy spent a few hours each day at his club. He needed time away from the constant stream of eager young suitors and he knew Georgiana was safe in Elizabeth's hands. While at his club, he had spoken to several friends who had been to the Frost Fair and they could not control their enthusiasm. The weather had turned so frigid for so long that the River Thames was frozen over. Darcy thought the idea of being able to walk across the Thames was an experience not to be missed. They could also partake of various amusements as well as enjoying hot food and beverages.

Even with the frequent callers, after Georgiana's debut the Darcys were all more relaxed. One morning as they ate breakfast together, Darcy looked up from his newspaper. "How would you ladies like to attend the Frost Fair?"

"What is the Frost Fair?" Both Elizabeth and Georgiana asked at the same time.

"I am not surprised you have not heard about it. You two have had no time to think about anything except the party. Now that it is happily in the past, I thought we could all use some amusement. Although it is still frightfully cold, if we dress properly, we should be fine. For the first time in anyone's memory, the River Thames is frozen solid. At the Frost Fair there are tents on the ice where you can purchase food and drinks, booths selling toys and trinkets, various performers, as well as skating. Sometime this week, someone is planning to walk an elephant across the Thames near Blackfriars Bridge."

"Is it truly safe? It sounds fascinating, but I have no wish to fall into the freezing water of the Thames," said Elizabeth.

"Since you weigh considerably less than an elephant, I feel confident that the only water you will be in that day is your bath!" Elizabeth joined them as they laughed at her fearful response. She was usually the first one to try something new and exciting but when she heard that the Thames was frozen, she thought about perishing in the icy river. *How can I consider doing something that could prevent me from ever holding Bennet again? I will never do anything to leave William without a mother for his son.*

"William, do they hold the Frost Fair every year? Perhaps Bennet will be able to experience a Frost Fair when he is old enough."

"It is difficult to say. There are plans in place to erect a new London Bridge which will allow the water to flow more easily. A new bridge will be less likely to allow the ice to build up, but that construction is still in the planning stage. The other factor is the weather; no one knows when we will have another frigidly cold winter."

"Well, I cannot wait to go! I shall be able to tell everyone that I saw an elephant walk across the Thames!"

"Yes, Georgie, it will be quite the story to tell. Shall we plan to go tomorrow?" A gleeful Georgiana Darcy clapped her approval of her brother's suggestion while Elizabeth forced a smile.

That night, as Elizabeth and Darcy prepared for bed, he took her hand and led her to the settee in front of the fireplace. The fire was roaring, and the room was quite comfortable despite the frigid temperature outside.

"Elizabeth, what is it that has you so ill at ease? Is it the Frost Fair or something else? You have not been the same since we spoke about tomorrow's excursion at breakfast."

"I read the article in the newspaper and I know that hundreds of people are walking on the frozen river every day. I do not know why but my first thought was what would happen if I fell through the ice. I could only think about never seeing the people I love again."

"Every day we are all together is a gift. None of us knows what day will be our last and so we must live every day to its fullest. I would never do anything that could possibly put you or Georgiana or Ben, in any danger. I would give my life and all I possess to keep the three of you safe. Do you believe me, my love?"

"Of course I believe you and I do not know why I am reacting this way. You should not be surprised to hear that I was the most adventurous of my sisters. I suppose now that I am married and have a child, my only thoughts are to be here to care for and love you and our son as long as possible. I am looking forward to going tomorrow and I am glad that Georgiana will have something new to speak to her callers about." Elizabeth and Darcy smiled and when they got into bed, she clung to her husband with increased urgency. She could not fall asleep, all she thought about was never returning home from the Frost Fair. *I love my son more than I ever realized I could love anyone. Ben is a baby and he needs his mother every day. William is the most wonderful husband and we are so happy together. How can I think about enjoying myself when I could lose everything important to me by falling through the ice? Elizabeth Bennet Darcy, you are a strong woman and William will never allow anything to harm you. If I return safely, I will have lots to write to Jane about it. I must think positively, and all will be well.*

THE FOLLOWING AFTERNOON, WHEN THE DARCYS returned from the Frost Fair, they were talking and laughing and gesturing about all the astonishing sights they had just seen. They were all amazed at the many wonders on the ice, the variety of foods for sale and the crowded drinking tents where you could purchase rum or grog. They stopped into a tent to warm up and purchased hot chocolate and tea. As they walked around the Fair, Darcy had not been surprised that his wife held onto his arm with both hands. Of course, the highlight of the day was the thrill of seeing an elephant walk across the River Thames. A story they would all retell many, many times over the following years.

CHAPTER 16

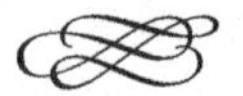

Unlike his usual feelings of dread before attending a party, Darcy was actually looking forward to attending the ball at the home of Lord and Lady Townsend. He had gone to school with the Townsend's eldest son, Viscount Paxton, and was looking forward to seeing his old friend for the first time in many years. On the afternoon of the party, Georgiana asked that she be excused from attending, she was not feeling well and was still tired from the weeks leading up to her big night. Elizabeth and Darcy assured her that they would be more than willing to send their regrets, but she told them that all she needed was some rest. They understood her feelings and went to the party without her.

As he had promised his mother, Richard also attended the Townsend's party. He was standing with his cousins when he noticed that Lady Emily was also there, looking very unhappy. He and the Darcys walked over to speak to her and they could sense that she seemed uneasy.

Their conversation was superficial and meaningless, and Richard was frustrated. He had dreamt about encountering Lady Emily in London and here he was, standing before her and unable to speak about anything except the weather. A moment later they understood why she was not more forthcoming when they were approached by two people whom Emily introduced as her parents. When Mrs. Carter heard Emily introduce Richard Fitzwilliam, she looked up and asked, "are *you* related to Lord and Lady Matlock?"

"Indeed madam, I am delighted to say that they are my parents and aunt and uncle to the Darcys."

Emily's mother was suddenly much more interested in meeting Richard, she smiled coyly while asking "are you the viscount, sir?"

Her mother is the most obvious social climber I have ever seen and that includes Caroline Bingley. She seemed impressed by the Darcys because she knows of their wealth, their enormous estate and their connections to my family.

"My older brother, Arthur, holds the title of Viscount Ashford; he and his wife are not in attendance this evening. They are currently residing at Matlock

House where his wife is entering her confinement." Richard made it clear to Mrs. Carter that his older brother was not on the market for a wife. When she heard that the Viscount was already married and about to have a child, Mrs. Carter's face immediately showed the disdain at meeting the *second* son. Her disappointment at hearing that another young, wealthy man with a title was not in need of a wife was easy to read on her face.

Looking down her nose she asked, "and where is it that you reside, Mr. Fitzwilliam."

"I have a large estate in Kent called Rosings Park which was left to me by my cousin." He did not want Emily's parents to think he was without assets.

"I met Mr. and Mrs. Darcy and Mr. Fitzwilliam several times in Derbyshire while I was staying at the rectory. Mr. Darcy bestowed the living at Kympton to Peter," Emily offered as a way to explain her acquaintance.

Despite his connection to the Darcys, Mr. Carter quickly surmised that a gentleman farmer was clearly not good enough to waste spending another moment with. "It was nice meeting you all, pray excuse us." Emily's father said as he led his wife and daughter away from Richard, Elizabeth and Darcy. Her father's firm hold on her arm did not permit her from doing anything other than being pulled away from a group of people she knew she might enjoy speaking to. Although she knew her father would brook no argument as he led her away, she looked back over her shoulder and smiled at Richard and the Darcys.

"Well, now I understand how she wound up married to that good for nothing Howard," Richard said dejectedly.

"Lady Emily is a grown woman of independent means. She is now old enough to make her own decisions and marry whomever she chooses. Although you are not the viscount, you are a wealthy man in your own right, and you would make any woman you chose a wonderful husband."

"Thank you for the recommendation, Lizzy. I just wish it was that easy."

She teasingly asked, "have I seen you ask her to dance yet? Remember how we spoke about courting her?"

"I would like to ask her to dance but I fear her mother might bite my head off if I come near them again."

"You will never know if you do not try," Darcy suggested. "Are you not the man who bravely fought the enemy to within an inch of his life in Spain? Where is that courage now?" Darcy tried to sound light hearted, but Richard knew his cousin was encouraging him to confront his new enemy, Mr. and Mrs. Carter.

He turned away from his cousins and walked directly toward where the Carters were standing. Richard bowed before her and asked, "Lady Howard, may I have the honor of dancing the next set with you?" Her mother had already warned her *not* to refuse any gentleman's request for a dance. She knew very well that if she refused one man, she would not be able to dance with anyone else. Her mother had told her several times that day that there would be many titled young men in attendance who might be looking for a wife.

Lady Emily did not look at her parents as she placed her hand on Richard's arm. "I would be very happy to dance with you, Mr. Fitzwilliam." She smiled at her parents as they walked to the dance floor. Many other couples were lining up to wait for the music to begin and Richard and Lady Emily stood opposite each other smiling. They were both hoping that their dance partner could not hear or feel how quickly their hearts were beating in anticipation of their first dance together.

When the music began, they started moving with the other couples, but they uttered only a few meaningless words to each other. When Richard garnered the courage to look into her eyes, he thought Lady Emily was looking back at him with some affection. *Does*

Emily have feelings for me or am I imagining things? I will not say or do anything to promote our relationship tonight, not with her mother watching us like the vulture she is. How did my dearest, sweetest Emily come from those horrible people? I will call on her tomorrow and ask her to take a walk with me. I must have some time alone with her, so we can speak honestly with each other without being observed by her parents.

Lord and Lady Matlock were standing near the dance floor when they saw their son dancing with Lady Howard. "Well, Hugh, perhaps you were correct when you said Richard reacted strongly to the mention of Lady Howard's name. She is a lovely young woman, yes, very lovely indeed."

"Patricia, do not get involved. I know that look on your face; I will acknowledge that perhaps I read Richard's reaction to hearing her name correctly, but I do not think we should interfere in any way."

"I suppose you are correct, my dear. Richard appears to have the situation well in hand." Lord Matlock smiled at his wife, kissed her hand and told her that he was going to speak to Darcy about Catherine.

Lord Matlock found his nephew standing alone and frowning while watching the dancers; more precisely watching Elizabeth dancing with someone he did not know. "Darcy, I am glad to find you alone; I wish to speak to you about my sister."

"Of course, let us move to a more private space to discuss this topic." The men moved to an alcove where they could not be overheard.

"Well, my boy, you were absolutely correct. My sister has completely lost her mind. She is so full of hatred for everyone and everything that she stares at the walls and talks to herself all day. I spoke with her maid and housekeeper and they confirmed what I saw myself."

"Do you have a plan to deal with her? I will never allow her to come near my family again. Her behavior is nothing but hurtful and I will have no part of her."

"I have taken care of everything. Your aunt and several companions have already left London. Patricia inherited a small estate near the sea in Dorset from her aunt and Catherine will live there for the remainder of her life. After examining her, Dr. Dawson, my physician, has sent along several cases of a tonic that should soothe her nerves."

"Do you think we will ever see Lady Catherine again?"

"It saddens me to say that I do not believe we will." Lord Matlock paused before continuing, "I thank you for bringing her behavior to my attention. Since coming to London, she has sequestered herself and did not respond to any of the invitations we sent her.

We thought she was still mourning Anne, but obviously it was much more than that."

"I am sorry my coming to you has brought you so much pain, but it will be better for everyone this way." He and his uncle embraced and walked back toward the party.

Darcy introduced his wife to Viscount Paxton, the son of Lord and Lady Townsend. "Mrs. Darcy, what a great pleasure to meet you. Many of Darcy's friends sincerely doubted he would *ever* marry."

"Viscount Paxton, it is a pleasure to meet you. William has told me a great deal about your days together at school. As to him not marrying, when you last saw him, he had not yet met me." Everyone laughed and continued to enjoy each other's company.

After Richard and Emily's set, he walked her back to her parents. When she removed her hand from his arm, he bowed and walked away with a big smile on his face.

The following day, Darcy, Elizabeth and Georgiana were sitting together at the breakfast table, each reading the letters which had arrived that morning. Elizabeth was reading a letter from Jane and was unconsciously shaking her head. "What has you so puzzled this morning, my love?"

"Puzzled? Why would you think I was puzzled?"

"Lizzy, we both saw you shaking your head as you were reading Jane's letter," Georgiana added.

"Let me tell you what my sister wrote, and I am certain you will both be shaking your heads. She writes that Caroline has not left Derbyshire since arriving before Christmas. She told Jane and Charles that she has no interest in returning to Town for the Season. It seems that she frequently takes their carriage to Kympton to help distribute food and clothing to the neediest in the parish. She has also been called on by Mr. Carter on a regular basis. She has spoken to Jane more than once about her feelings for him and asked Jane how she knew she was in love with Charles. Jane feels that Caroline is not the same woman she was before she came to the Harvest Ball." Elizabeth looked up to see two very perplexed faces listening to her recount Jane's message.

"Caroline Bingley is in love with Mr. Carter?" Georgiana was incredulous. "She chased after William for so long, I cannot imagine she would ever settle for a vicar. He is a fine man but not the type of person any of us could imagine Miss Bingley being attracted to. In the past, she has only thrown herself at very wealthy or titled men."

"I agree with Georgie, and if I were reading Jane's

letter, I believe I would have been shaking my head as well." They all laughed at Darcy's observation.

"Whatever happens, I hope both of them will be very happy. I am going up to the nursery for a few minutes," Elizabeth said as she rose from the table. She wanted to spend more time with her precious son before callers, once again, began arriving at Darcy House.

Later that morning, Richard walked the short distance between Matlock House and the Carter's townhouse on Grosvenor Square. As he neared his destination, he saw someone with whom he was acquainted leaving the Carter's home. *So, Lord Hedley, is now courting Lady Emily. Hedley, the degenerate womanizer and gambler whose parents have always lived too lavishly. They probably insist their son marry wealth to shore up their depleted family coffers and produce an heir. I am sure that Lord Hedley's mother and Mrs. Carter believe Lady Emily would fill the role well. Now I understand why her parents were so short with me last night – they are saving their sacrificial daughter for another miscreant with a title. I always hoped that I would have a good relationship with my future in-laws but maybe I need to take a page out of Darcy's book. Keep my in-laws as far away from Rosings as possible. We will see them only on special occasions and at the birth of our children. Slow down, Richard - that was a big leap – from calling on Lady Emily for the first time to celebrating the birth of our children. I cannot stop myself, I feel a warm contentedness come over me just thinking about a happy future with my lovely Emily.*

Richard waited until Lord Hedley was far out of sight and he was quickly admitted to the Carter's home. As he entered, he encountered Lady Emily donning her outerwear. "Lady Howard, I am very happy to see you today. Has my arrival kept you from leaving for an appointment?"

"I was hoping to take in some fresh air and walk in Hyde Park. Would you care to join me?"

"Thank you, Lady Howard, I would be delighted."

As they left the house, she took Richard's proffered arm; the footman accompanying them was thoughtful enough to walk a good distance behind them. They walked in silence for several minutes before Lady Emily began the conversation. "Last night, you told my parents that you live on an estate that you recently inherited. May I ask what you did before taking over the estate?"

"As a second son, there were few vocations open to me and unlike your brother, I knew I was not cut out for the Church. I was a member of His Majesty's Army for many years and planned to spend my entire career in the Army. When I enlisted, I refused to allow my father to purchase a commission for me; I believed the men under my command would respect their leader more if they knew that I had earned my rank. I entered the army as a young recruit and through my work as a regimental leader while engaged in battle, in time I was fortunate to earn the rank of Colonel on my own."

"Did you leave His Majesty's Army when you inherited your estate?"

"Not exactly. Two years ago, I was seriously injured by a bullet in my leg. While still in Spain, the Army doctors determined that my injury was too serious to allow me to return to the battlefield. Shortly after returning to London, my cousin, Anne, died and left her family's estate to me. I had always thought of myself as a soldier; leading my men into battle and fighting beside them. When I was here in London to recuperate, my commanders confirmed what the Army doctors had diagnosed; I was finished with the war. When I was well enough, I would be assigned to training recruits, a position which held no appeal to me. When I came into my inheritance, I resigned my commission and have been learning how to be a gentleman farmer, a role I never thought I would play. My only connection to my time in His Majesty's army is my damaged leg which still aches terribly when it rains or I attempt to walk too quickly."

"Thank you for sharing your story with me, Colonel."

"That is a title I no longer hold; I am Mister Fitzwilliam now. I never thought it would happen, but I have come to enjoy a life where no one is trying to shoot me." Richard laughed and looked at Lady Emily, who was smiling.

"I am very happy that you are out of harm's way."

"May I call on you tomorrow and perhaps walk in the park, again?"

"Yes, Mr. Fitzwilliam, I look forward to it."

CHAPTER 17

The next morning Richard arrived at the Carter's townhouse hoping he and Lady Emily could once again speak openly as they walked together. When the footman opened the door, Richard was delighted to see her standing nearby as if she anticipated his arrival and they quickly left the house. He was encouraged that Lady Emily cared enough about him that she wanted to protect him from any interaction with her parents. As they exited the Carter townhouse, again followed by a footman, Lady Emily took Richard's arm before he offered it and he was heartened by her action. She looked up at him and asked him, "May I speak openly, Mr. Fitzwilliam?" He nodded his acquiescence. "I believe that you hold me in some affection, and I must tell you I feel affection for you as well." He smiled contentedly as he placed his other hand on top of hers. "However, I wish to be honest when I tell you that I have never been in love. I fear I do not know if I am capable of loving you or anyone else. I would like you to know the truth about my marriage. May I tell you my story?"

He stopped walking and looked at the woman on his arm. "I wish to know everything about you my dear Lady Emily. If telling me of your marriage will bring you pain, I pray you would spare yourself."

"If I ever cared for my husband, perhaps it would be a painful story. Since that is not the case, pray allow me to proceed." Again, he nodded his agreement and they resumed walking. "Ours was a marriage in name only. Lord Howard needed an heir and a wife with a large dowry. His parents presented many eligible young women of the *ton* to him, but he was not attracted to any of them. We met several seasons ago and since I was not interested in him, he decided that I would be perfect as his wife. Marrying me would allow him to continue his wastrel ways using my dowry money. He told me that he only needed me to produce a son and then he would no longer come to my bed.

"I was miserably unhappy, he barely said ten words a day to me while we were living in the same house. A few months after our marriage I realized that I was with child. I was elated that I would have a baby to love and love me in return. Sadly, before I felt the quickening, the child was lost. My husband was disappointed, but he quickly recovered from his melancholy and resumed his nightly drinking, gambling and visits to his favorite brothel.

"Leaving a gambling hall one night, he was walking back to our townhouse when he was confronted by some criminals. He had had too much to drink and when he refused to give them money, one of them pushed him down. He was quite drunk and easily lost his balance, falling and hitting his head on a paving stone. The robbers left him there on the sidewalk to die but not before taking all his money and his gold pocket watch."

"Thank you for telling me the truth." Richard paused before saying, "you have been terribly mistreated by the very people who should have been caring for your welfare."

"I thank you for saying that Mr. Fitzwilliam."

He looked at her face and simply smiled for her to continue. "I was forced to marry Lord Howard despite my protestations to my parents that there was a total lack of affection on both our parts. My parents insisted that I marry him, bear an heir and then we could both go our separate ways. When I asked my mother, 'what of love? I wish to marry for love or at least some mutual affection.' My mother told me that very few marriages are a love match, and most unions in the *ton* are marriages of convenience. She added, 'do some arranged marriages ultimately lead to love? I suppose some do, but when dealing with the nobility, marriages are arranged to benefit the families involved.' And that is how I became Lady Howard."

"I appreciate you sharing your story. I believe that you and I can marry for love and have a wonderful life together. It is too soon for me to ask for your hand but rest assured that I will do everything necessary to have you as my wife." Richard turned to Lady Emily and gazed into her eyes. He was now certain that she looked at him with affection and maybe even love. He took her hand and raised it to his lips. Richard saw a small smile on her face when he kissed her hand.

He looked back and saw the footman a good distance behind them, but he wondered if the servant would feel obligated to tell Mr. Carter that Richard had kissed his daughter's hand. "I must ask you something before we return. I saw Lord Hedley leaving your house shortly before I arrived yesterday. Must I challenge him to a duel to eliminate his pursuit of your hand?"

She laughed, "no duel will be necessary, sir. My father had Hedley investigated and learned that his Lordship is deeply in debt. He would not only require all my settlement money and what is left of my dowry, but much of my parents' money, as well. My father has worked hard his entire life and is now a successful exporter of farm products. My parents will stop at almost nothing to have another son in-law with a title *except* lose a farthing of their hard-earned fortune. You need not worry about Lord Hedley ever darkening my door again. I heard my father instructing the staff that he was not to be admitted to our home under any circumstances."

"I am delighted to hear that I shall not have to challenge him to a duel. Shall we walk back now?"

"Yes, we should; I have most certainly been out too long. I do not wish to give my parents any reason to keep me from spending more time with you." Lady Emily smiled at Richard as they slowly walked back to the Carter's home. "Shall we walk again tomorrow morning? Now that the fog has lifted, I would like to enjoy as much fresh air as possible."

"I would like to, but I must return to Kent on the morrow; I have obligations to my estate. I only came to London for my cousin, Georgiana Darcy's debut, and planned to leave soon after. Since seeing you at the Townsend's Ball earlier this week, I have remained in Town in the hope of spending more time with you. I would like you to visit Rosings someday, someday soon. The house is too big by half, but the grounds are quite beautiful."

"I would like to see Rosings," Lady Emily blushed as she responded.

"And so, you shall, my lady." Richard and Emily both smiled as they walked up the front steps of her parent's home. "May I write to you? There must be a way that we can communicate."

After thinking a moment, she said, "I have a good friend from my finishing school days who lives in Kent. Her name is Mary Greenley. If you write to me using her name, my parents will not think to examine your letters."

"I could have used your keen skills of subterfuge while I was fighting Napoleon," Richard said with a laugh. "Farewell, Lady Emily, until we meet again."

"Please call me Emily and may I call you Richard?" Richard nodded his agreement and smiled and then she added, "farewell, Miss Greenley. I hope to hear from you soon." Emily turned and walked through the front door as Richard strode away whistling a happy tune.

~

WHEN RICHARD RETURNED TO ROSINGS IN MARCH, HE told Mrs. Elkins about his desire to communicate with a friend and asked his housekeeper to address his letters to Lady Emily. Mrs. Elkins was happy to comply and Richard's letters to Lady Emily were never looked at with anything but happiness by her parents; Mary Greenley was really Lady Mary and the daughter of a peer.

He received a letter from Lady Emily shortly after he returned to Kent. He wrote back telling her of his plans for the spring planting and some improvements being made to the tenants' homes. In his first response, Richard did not want to write of anything personal in fear that his letter might be intercepted. In turn, Emily wrote of some parties she had attended at the homes of various friends and she described who had called on the Carters and with whom she drank tea.

DURING THE REMAINDER OF THE SEASON, THE DARCYS attended a few well-chosen social events and in April, they happily returned to Pemberley. Bennet was almost six months old and they wanted their son to get to know Pemberley as he became more and more aware of his surroundings. They were all relieved that Georgiana's successful entrance into London society was behind them. She told her brother and sister that she enjoyed dancing and speaking with the young men who sought her out at the parties they attended. These same young men often called on her at Darcy House, but she told her brother and sister that she had not met anyone special.

SHORTLY AFTER RETURNING TO DERBYSHIRE, CATHERINE and David were very happy to greet them all at Winthrope Hall. Their new baby, Jane Elizabeth Brooks was a beautiful blonde baby who always seemed to be smiling.

The day after they arrived at Winthrope Hall, Elizabeth and Georgiana were walking together in the gardens. Georgiana kept looking at her sister, "Georgie, is something wrong? Do I have something on my face?"

"I do not know how to say this but, how could you ever imagine yourself married to Lord Winthrope? He is so different from William. Lizzy, I am so glad you married my brother."

"I believe I have already explained to you how sad and lonely I was. David Brooks came into my life when I was vulnerable and filled some of the void in my life."

"He is married to your sister! Does that bother you?"

"Catherine and David are very much in love and I am so glad they found each other. Brooks is married to someone who loves him the way a wife should love her husband. If I had married him, I know neither of us would be as happy as we are now." Elizabeth stopped walking and faced her sister. "Georgie, I am the happiest woman in England because I married your brother. He is the very best man I have ever known, and I am thankful every day that I have William, Ben and you." Elizabeth embraced her sister with tears of joy in her eyes. "You need not worry about any of the choices I have made. Everything has worked out precisely as it should." Elizabeth and Georgiana walked arm in arm to join the others in the house.

~

RICHARD AND LADY EMILY WROTE EACH OTHER regularly throughout the spring and into the summer. In May, he received another letter from Lady Emily telling him of her summer plans. She was returning to Suffolk with her parents in May and she was looking forward to spending the summer at her family's estate near the sea. Richard enjoyed hearing from Emily but was somewhat frustrated by the lack of anything meaningful in her letters until a message he received in July.

July 8, 1814

Carter House

Suffolk

My dear Lady Mary,

I have been spending a lot of time thinking about what you have written in your letters. I have often thought about what we discussed on the days we walked together in Hyde Park; you spoke about us being happy together. I enjoyed being in your company in Derbyshire and London and learning a little more about you through your letters. I believe an invitation to the Greenley estate in Kent may help us get to know each other better and determine if we are well suited. I can travel with Maggie, my trusted maid, and your housekeeper can welcome me before entering your home. Your staff can unload my trunks, and no one will be the wiser. My driver and coachman can begin their journey back to Suffolk and remain there until I write my parents about the requested date of my return. Please, Mary, I hope you will invite me soon.

Your caring friend,

Emily

Richard was especially anxious about his response to Emily's letter about her visit to Rosings Park. He did not want *this* particular letter to be intercepted after one of her parents observed another envelope addressed to their daughter from Mary Greenley.

My dearest friend,

I cannot express how eagerly I am looking forward to your upcoming visit. Please let me know when you plan to arrive.

Until we meet again,

I remain your obedient servant,

Mary

As Lady Emily and her mother sat at the breakfast table at their Suffolk estate, Mrs. Carter noticed her daughter reading a letter with a smile on her face. "What has Lady Mary written that has you so amused?"

"I have the most wonderful news, Mama. Lady Mary

and her parents have invited me to visit their estate in Kent next month."

"Emily, that *is* good news. I am certain that Lord and Lady Greenley will also invite other nobility to their house party; that is what those people do. They invite other peers to their homes and then they reciprocate. They spend the entire summer going from one house party to the next. This trip is a wonderful opportunity for you to meet someone to marry. You *are* a widow and not getting any younger; I look forward to hearing your reports from Kent. Just remember to keep an open mind."

"Yes, Mother, I promise to keep an open mind and carefully consider all my options."

"Is it not curious that Lady Mary never wrote to you before, but since the winter she has become a frequent correspondent."

"I ran into Lady Mary while we were in London and we decided that too much time had lapsed without us seeing or hearing from each other. We decided that day at the milliners that we would write to each other more often. We were very close friends at school and there is really no reason that we cannot be close friends again."

Mrs. Carter raised her tea cup, "here's to a successful visit to Kent!"

"Yes, to a successful visit to Kent!"

CHAPTER 18

Elizabeth was looking forward to once again attending the Bingleys' Summer Ball. It was at their party two years prior when her husband expressed his love for her and had, once again, asked her to marry him. During their time together that night they shared what was in their hearts. Not long after the Bingley's party, they were joined in marriage.

The Darcys traveled to Birchwood Manor on the morning of the Ball and planned to stay over one night before returning to Pemberley and their son. Georgiana accompanied them and when she entered the ballroom, she was surprised to see that several of the men who had called on her in London were in attendance.

Georgiana was speaking with Jane and Charles when she was happily surprised to see David Arlington walking toward her. "Good evening, Mr. and Mrs.

Bingley, Miss Darcy." He bowed before them and when he stood up, he looked at Georgiana, "Miss Darcy, may I have the pleasure of dancing the next set with you?"

"Mr. Arlington, I look forward to it."

"Excellent, I will return shortly."

While he walked away, Georgiana hoped he could not feel her eyes following him until he was lost in the crowd. "I did not realize you knew Mr. Arlington. His family's estate is not far from here," Jane said.

"We met at my Ball at Darcy House, but he did not call on me during the remainder of our time in London."

"Are you happy to see him? Charles has met with David's brother a few times to discuss some farming issues. He told Charles that David has been spending more and more time here since they lost both their parents in the past few months. Charles said he was very impressed with the family. They have lived in Derbyshire for a hundred years or more and they are very generous to their tenants."

"I am terribly sorry to hear of his loss, I had no idea. I am happy to see him but since he never called on me, I did not think I would ever see him again. I am a bit surprised that he asked me to dance."

A few minutes later, David Arlington came to escort her to the dance floor and they did not speak for the first few minutes of the set. In due time he asked, "how do you like living in Derbyshire? Do you like to ride? Do you prefer London over the countryside?"

Georgiana thought it inappropriate to offer her condolences while they danced. She responded to his questions as they went through the steps, "I love being at Pemberley more than anywhere else in the world. I love being in the country, watching the seasons change and helping my sister in all her efforts to care for our tenants." When the dance was ended, he walked her back to the Bingleys, bowed and walked away before she could tell him how sorry she was about his parents.

After the next dance set was finished, Caroline was standing with her brother and sister when Peter Carter approached them. "Mr. and Mrs. Bingley, my compliments on your lovely party. I am grateful to have been invited."

"We are very happy that you were able to join us, Mr. Carter," Jane said as she smiled.

"Miss Bingley, may I request your next available set?"

"Thank you; I am free to dance the next."

"Wonderful, the musicians are warming up now; shall we join the others?"

Caroline placed her hand on Peter Carter's arm and could feel her heart racing. Jane looked at Charles and they both smiled. She had told her husband everything she had observed and her conversations with Caroline. As she was walking toward the dance floor, Caroline thought, *why am I so nervous about dancing with him? Will he say something this evening that will reveal how he feels about me? Do I love him? We have been spending so much time together and I enjoy being with him, but…it is just a dance Caroline, not a marriage proposal! What if Peter Carter did propose, what would I say?*

As they stood opposite each other, he smiled at Caroline and she knew then that she would accept his proposal, *if* it ever came to be. "Will you remain in Derbyshire for the remainder of the summer, Miss Bingley?"

"Yes, I have no plans to leave. I find I like being here and spending time with Jane, Charles and Maddie. I have enjoyed my time helping you in Kympton; it is very gratifying work." *Stop talking Caroline and let the man say something!*

"I have also enjoyed the time we have spent together helping my parishioners and also during my calls to Birchwood Manor." She smiled at his words and then turned to follow the steps of the dance. When the set ended, he asked her if she would care to go out to the terrace for some fresh air. "I am sure there will be many others out there enjoying the cool evening, so we need not worry about any impropriety."

"Thank you, that sounds lovely."

When they walked out to the terrace, they saw that there were many others enjoying the evening air but they were far enough away from anyone else that their conversation could not be overheard. "It is so lovely out here. While they were on their wedding trip, Charles and Jane stopped at Birchwood to inspect the property before deciding to buy it. They have made many improvements and are very happy living here."

"I can understand why, it is a lovely estate." Neither of them said anything more for several minutes and then Peter said, "Miss Bingley, I would like to tell you how much I have come to look forward to spending time with you. I know you are a lady of the *ton,* but I wish to know how you feel about being away from London society. I suppose what I am clumsily trying to ask is if you thought you could be happy living in the country all year."

Caroline's dreams of a life with Peter were becoming a reality. "Yes, Mr. Carter, my answer is yes. I no longer have any desire to return to my old life in London and all that entails." *Can it be true? He loves me and intends to marry me. I am happier than I ever imagined I could be!*

Peter stepped toward Caroline and kissed her hand

without taking his eyes off her. "Will you enter into a formal courtship with me, Miss Bingley?"

"Very happily, sir, very happily indeed."

"My dearest, Miss Bingley, I…"

"Will you not call me Caroline?"

"Yes, of course, and you must call me Peter when we are alone."

"You were saying?"

"Ah, yes, I was saying, my dearest Caroline, I will speak to your brother tonight and obtain his permission."

"If you do not mind, I would like to keep our courtship to ourselves. I have reached my majority and can make my own decisions." Caroline did not wish to make their understanding public. She feared Peter would change his mind if he knew the truth about her past behavior and she wanted to spare herself the humiliation that ending their courtship would bring her. She hesitated before she continued, "there is something I must tell you before our relationship goes any farther."

"I am ready to listen although I do not think you can tell me anything that could change my feelings for you."

"Thank you, but I did not always behave as a kind person should." Caroline raised her hand to stop

Peter from objecting. She knew that she needed to clear her conscience before she could ever think about accepting his proposal of marriage. "The truth is that before I met you, I was a mean-spirited, social climbing shrew. I did not treat people as I should; I spoke to servants as if they did not merit me being civil with them. In an attempt to lower Mrs. Darcy's worth in the eyes of Mr. Darcy, I criticized her every move before they were married. At the time, I was determined to marry him myself; not because I loved him but because of his wealth and the elevated social standing he represented. In his defense, Mr. Darcy was never anything more than polite to me and never encouraged me to pursue him in any way."

Caroline paused to gather her thoughts, "I know I am not the woman I was last year. Since coming here and meeting you at the Harvest Ball I know I have changed. I have tried to be a better person, to listen to others and try to understand their feelings. In the past, I judged everyone by only thinking about how knowing them might benefit me; improve my status in the *ton* or help me meet a suitable husband. You and you alone are responsible for the changes I have made. I happily confess, I like myself much better than I ever did before; I am so deeply ashamed of my previous behavior.

"After our conversation at Christmas, I spoke to my maid about donating my gowns to the church; you were correct, she told me she had been selling them and sending the extra money to her family. I told her that I wanted her to continue to do so and I also apologized to her for the many years I have treated her so poorly. Happily, she accepted my apology and told me she would like to stay with me, although in the past she confessed she had looked for another position whenever I had been especially cruel to her." Caroline looked at Peter as he reached out to take her hand in his. "If you would like to change your mind about our courtship, I will completely understand. No one else knows about our agreement, nor does anyone ever need to know."

Caroline was close to tears when Peter said, "let us return to the ballroom, I am eager to dance with you again." He kissed Caroline's hand again before escorting her back to the ballroom. "Whoever you were before we met does not concern me in the least. I believe that life in the *ton* demands women behave in precisely the way you described. I am happy to say that I never met the 'old' Caroline Bingley; I am in love with the woman I met at Pemberley last year. Now, my dear, may I anticipate dancing another set with you this evening?"

"Two sets in one night, people will talk," she teased.

"I care not what others think; only your wishes concern me."

"Thank you for accepting me as I am now, I will do everything in my power to be the person who deserves your love." Peter smiled as they returned to the ballroom.

"In that case, a second set sounds perfect; perhaps the supper set or the last set?"

"Perhaps both?" Caroline and Peter looked at each other and smiled. Jane saw them enter the ballroom and observed their happy faces. If they had come to some sort of understanding, she could not be happier for her sister and was anxious to speak to Charles about what she had just seen.

As they had for the last two years, Darcy and Elizabeth danced the first set together at the Bingley's Ball. After the second set was well underway, they spoke to some friends before Darcy followed Elizabeth out to the terrace. "The air on a summer night has a wonderful stillness to it."

"Mr. Darcy, what a lovely observation." Those were the same words they uttered on the night two years prior when he proposed to Elizabeth again.

"More than anything, I wanted to take you in my arms that night and never let you go. My love for you was almost too powerful for me to control."

"Perhaps if my sister had not interrupted us, I would have agreed to be your wife that night; I was still so confused about my feelings. I kept thinking that if I opened my heart to you as I did in Hertfordshire, I would lose you once again. I knew I could not endure my heart being broken a second time as it was when we thought you were dead."

Darcy embraced his wife and quietly said, "hush, my love. I am not going anywhere. I will never, never leave you and you will be forced to live with your grumpy husband for many, many years to come. Did I tell you how much I love you, Mrs. Darcy?"

"Your secret is safe with me, Mr. Darcy." She was in the arms of the man she loved, feeling the power of their love as she had when he proposed to her on this same terrace. They kissed briefly and looked at each other with the knowledge they were both thinking the same thing. "I hate to leave Jane and Charles' party early but I am feeling rather fatigued."

"I am very sorry to hear that. I will be happy to escort you to your quarters and make sure you are comfortably settled in your bed."

"I do appreciate your care and concern for my well-being. Shall we go?" Elizabeth smiled as she took Darcy's arm and they both moved as quickly as possible through the ballroom and toward the stairs. He stopped to speak to a footman while Elizabeth continue to walk up the steps. When he joined her on the landing she asked, "what did you speak to him about?"

"I told him that my wife was feeling unwell and I was escorting her to her chambers. He asked if I needed anything and I assured him that I am fully capable to seeing to your needs. If a doctor is needed, I will let him know."

"Well done, sir. Your serious demeanor allows you to get away with expressing thoughts in a manner that most of us would be too shy to say."

"Years of practice, my love, years of practice."

"In that case, I am becoming more unwell by the minute. We should make haste to my chambers."

"I am right behind you, vixen." Elizabeth laughed at her husband's teasing words as he chased her down the hallway toward their rooms.

WHEN JANE AND CHARLES FINALLY ENTERED THEIR chambers, they were both exhausted. Charles embraced his wife, "thank you, my wonderful Jane. The Ball was a huge success from start to finish!"

"Thank you for your praise but I did have a lot of help. Caroline took on a great deal of the responsibility and she was ever so helpful." Jane paused, "do you know anything about your sister and Peter Carter? I saw them enter the ballroom from the terrace and they both looked very happy."

"I saw them dancing together and talking a great deal. My sister is certainly old enough to make her own decisions, but I do not know anything more than you."

"I hope they find happiness together. Your sister is not the same person she was when she arrived unannounced before the Harvest Ball. Maybe meeting Peter Carter is the reason for the change in her behavior." Jane yawned, "I am sorry, but I must prepare for bed. Maddie will be awake before we know it."

"Good night, Jane. Sweet dreams, my love."

After the Ball at Birchwood Manor, Georgiana did not see David Arlington again. He had only danced with her once even though she did not dance every set. He did not offer her a refreshment when the dance ended. He escorted her back to her family but did not remain to speak with them. After being together at Birchwood Manor, he did not call on her at Pemberley. She wondered why his behavior toward her was so inconsistent. They got along quite well, had several interesting discussions, and enjoyed dancing together. But he did not make any attempt to see her again and she was, once again, determined to forget about him.

CHAPTER 19

KENT

Before leaving her family's estate, Lady Emily gave a great deal of thought to her planned journey. She knew it was completely improper and her reputation would be ruined if anyone learned of her stay in the home of an unmarried man. Richard was a man of the world and Emily had already been married. *Would Richard try to bed me when we are alone? No, he is a gentleman and knows about my terrible relationship with Lord Howard. How do I feel about him? Do I love him? Can I love anyone? I cannot answer those questions until I spend more time with him. No one need know the truth about my trip and if we are meant to be together, everyone will know soon enough.*

In August, Emily left Suffolk to visit Richard at Rosings Park. As she suggested in her letter, Richard awaited her arrival in the entrance hall while Mrs. Elkins stood on the front steps. When the Carter's carriage pulled up the drive to Rosings, her footman helped her exit the carriage. Mrs. Elkins stepped forward and curtsied before saying loudly enough for the driver and coachmen to hear, "welcome to Rosings Park, your Ladyship. Lord and Lady Greenley and Lady Mary are looking forward to greeting you in the drawing room." Richard's footmen quickly unloaded Lady Emily's trunks and the Carter's carriage was soon on its journey back to Ipswich.

When he saw Emily enter Rosings, his heart was beating so fast he thought that everyone could sense his anxiety. He approached the woman of his dreams and bowed before her and kissed her hand. "Welcome to Rosings Park, Lady Howard. Thank you, Mrs. Elkins for the efficiency of our guest's arrival. Lady Howard, would you care for some refreshments or would you prefer to go to your room and rest before tea?"

"Mr. Fitzwilliam, I thank you for your kind hospitality. I would like to go to my room to freshen up. I will join you for tea in an hour, if that is convenient?"

"Whatever you wish, my lady. I will see you in an hour." Richard smiled as Mrs. Elkins showed Emily to her suite of rooms. As she walked up the stairs, he saw Emily looking around at the décor and smiling. He was trying to stem his optimism; the woman he loved was in his home. *I know I want to propose while Emily is here, but I do not wish to ask her too soon. She has been hurt by so many people, I know she must come to trust me over the next few weeks. It is not proper for her to be here with me, but I want Emily beside me for the rest of my life; it is the only way for her to know me well enough to accept my proposal. Mrs. Elkins and my staff have assured me of their discretion.*

That evening after dinner, they were drinking tea in the drawing room. Emily had just played the pianoforte and sang for Richard. He already knew he loved her, but hearing her play and sing, he was certain she was the most remarkable woman he had ever met.

"I never asked you what you told your parents about your trip here."

"I was smiling when I read your response to my letter asking for an invitation to Rosings. My mother could not understand what Mary had written that was so amusing. I told her that the Greenleys had invited me to their estate in Kent. She told me that I would most likely meet many titled men there and I should 'keep my options open'. She reminded me that I had already been married once and was not getting any younger."

Richard shook his head at hearing Mrs. Carter's unkind remarks. "I will not dignify her words with a response. How did you grow up to be so wonderful when your parents are so cruel?"

"I cannot think of them as cruel; they are simply

blinded by their desire to raise our family's standing in the *ton.* They do not realize how hurtful some of their comments are."

"Pray, make no excuses for their horrible words. I already know they do not like me; they made that clear at the Townsend's Ball. I do not know if I can ever forgive them for the way they have treated you."

"Perhaps I would be more critical of them if my husband was still alive and I was still so desperately unhappy. I am ready to move on with my life and am looking forward to whatever comes next."

"As am I, Emily." They smiled at each other and Richard asked, "shall I escort you upstairs or would you rather have more tea?"

"I am feeling rather tired from my travels today; you need not escort me. I look forward to whatever you have planned for tomorrow. Good night, Richard."

Richard rose and kissed Emily's hand. "Good night, Emily. Happy dreams, my lady." Emily smiled at her host before she left the room.

Richard poured himself a brandy, sat down on the sofa and closed his eyes. *Things have gone very well today. Emily seems so happy to be here with me. I saw her taking note of the paintings, rugs and curtains. She can redecorate the entire house if she so desires. Slow down, Richard; today was her first day at Rosings. Do not do anything to scare her away or ask her to answer a question she is not ready for. I feel so happy to have Emily in my home and I hope before too long, it shall be her home as well. Watching her play and sing for me is like heaven on earth. I will do anything to win her hand!*

THE FIRST WEEK OF EMILY'S VISIT PASSED QUICKLY; Richard showed her all around his estate. They took the phaeton into the village of Hunsford and walked around some of the shops. They met Mr. and Mrs. Collins while they were out walking and Charlotte Collins invited them to return to the parsonage for some refreshments. They happily agreed to the plan and spent a relaxed half hour in the company of the gracious Mrs. Collins, her long-winded husband and Rebecca, their adorable little girl. Charlotte told Lady Emily that until they married, she and Elizabeth Darcy were best friends. Lady Emily spoke of her many meetings with the Darcys while she was living with her brother in Derbyshire. Lady Emily told the Collins' that she was visiting her friend when she met Mr. Fitzwilliam at a party. Charlotte did not question why Lady Howard and Richard were walking together and they did not volunteer any further information.

LADY EMILY AND RICHARD WERE SPENDING ALMOST ALL their time together; eating their meals together, walking in Rosings beautiful gardens, riding to some of Richard's favorite spots for a picnic and reading together in the Rosings library when the weather kept them indoors. While they were walking or dining, they spoke about anything and everything that came into their minds. They took turns asking questions about how they each felt about certain topics. By the second week of her visit, they both felt they had come to know each other very well. He told her the terms of his cousin Anne's will and how he had inherited her estate when Anne passed away. "Why did her mother not inherit Rosings upon her husband's death?"

"My aunt and uncle did not make a love match; they were often heard arguing loudly about the smallest things. Before his death, my uncle, Sir Louis DeBourgh wrote his will leaving Rosings to Anne when she reached the age of twenty-four. After my uncle's death, my aunt ran Rosings and even after her twenty fourth birthday, Anne was always sickly and she never felt strong enough to take over the responsibility. When she realized that her days were few, Anne wrote her own will, leaving Rosings to me. After Anne's death and after I resigned my commission, I came here and offered my aunt the opportunity to remain at Rosings and live in the dower house, but she adamantly refused. If you had ever met my aunt, you would understand that we could never live under the same roof. She angrily decamped to her townhouse in London vowing to never again return to Rosings or speak to me.

"My father recently wrote to me about my aunt. It seems she tried to intrude on Georgiana Darcy's debut ball. Darcy had received several letters expressing her ongoing displeasure with his marriage. She repeatedly told him him that marrying Elizabeth not only tainted the family tree, but also ruined any chance that Georgiana could make a good match. Darcy thought she might try to ruin the party, so he gave his staff specific instructions about what to do if she showed up. It seems that on the night of the ball, my aunt had to be physically carried out of the house by Darcy's footmen. When my father went to speak to his sister about her behavior, he found her staring at the wall and speaking to herself; it appears she has completely lost her mind. She was examined by my family's physician and rather than send her to Bedlam, she has been resettled in Dorset with a large staff to prevent her from hurting herself or anyone else."

"What a terrible turn of events for your aunt. Did she always behave this way, or do you think the death of her daughter caused her inappropriate behavior?"

"It is hard to say. My aunt never took 'no' for an answer. I wish her well, but I am relieved that Darcy and his family are safe. She was obsessed with destroying their family and now that threat has been removed."

"I am very fond of the Darcys and I am glad they do not feel threatened any longer." They walked quietly arm in arm, enjoying their compatibility. "How did you learn how to be the master of an estate? Surely, your experience in the army was not enough."

"My cousin Darcy has been an invaluable resource; whenever I have an estate problem I cannot solve, I write to him and he usually comes up with a viable solution. Darcy and I are closer than cousins; we grew up as brothers and spent every summer together either at Pemberley or Matlock Manor. He is a very good man and he and Elizabeth are very happy together. I will tell you their story at another time; for now, I believe it is time for us to change for dinner.

As they were out walking the following day, Richard said, "Emily you are a woman of many talents."

"What do you mean?"

"You ride well, you play and sing beautifully, and you are so easy to talk to. At a moment's notice, you came up with a clever idea of how we could correspond with each other. When I asked you to visit, you staged the entire affair. You traveled with a person you could trust, and you choreographed your arrival better than Wellington plans an attack. I wish I had met you sooner, I would have dressed you in a soldier's uniform and used you to plan our war strategies."

"I wish I had met you sooner, as well." Emily blushed and decided to change the topic as they continued to walk. "Will you tell me how Mr. and Mrs. Darcy came to be married?"

"It is an incredible story and I will try to shorten the tale that took more than a year to come to a happy conclusion." Richard told Emily of the Darcy family's connection to George Wickham and that Wickham believed that Darcy was responsible for the death of a woman whom he said he wanted to marry. "To exact revenge on Darcy, Wickham sought to hurt Darcy and anyone he loved in any way he could."

Richard recounted the details of how Wickham and Mrs. Younge schemed together and kidnapped Georgiana in Ramsgate. He became emotional when he told her how severely Darcy had been wounded by Wickham during his cousin's rescue. "It was the worst day of my life. Darcy is like a brother to me and for the first few hours after he was injured, I was certain that we would lose him."

"I will repeat the words you said to me in Hyde Park when I was telling you the story of my marriage; if it is too difficult to recount, please spare yourself the pain."

"I thank you for caring, but there is not much more. Before the kidnapping, Darcy had been in Hertfordshire helping Charles Bingley and it was there that Darcy and Elizabeth fell in love and became betrothed. The same morning he proposed, he received my express telling him of Georgiana's kidnapping and he left Hertfordshire immediately."

"We feigned Darcy's death to protect Elizabeth and Georgiana as long as Wickham was on the loose. I took Darcy to his estate in Scotland and arranged for his medical care. I went to the Bennet's estate and told Elizabeth that Darcy was dead. She eventually moved to Derbyshire to live with Jane and Charles Bingley.

"When Darcy recovered and we learned Wickham was dead, Darcy reunited with Elizabeth at Birchwood Manor and were married soon after. My cousin and his wife have had their love tested beyond all reason, but their marriage is a love match that I envy."

Lady Emily blushed and looked away, "Thank you for telling me. They appear so happy together, you could never imagine the hardships they have endured." They walked on for several minutes, "We have been walking for a long time; shall we return to the house for some refreshment?"

"Yes, that is a good idea."

THE FOLLOWING DAY, THEY WERE STROLLING THROUGH the formal gardens. "Richard, I want to speak to you about growing up in Suffolk and the events that have led me to be here with you."

"I thought you told me all about your family."

"Not everything. I feel I know you better now and want you to know the complete truth. My oldest brother, John, was the answer to my parents' prayers. They did not have children for many years after they were married and worried that they would never be blessed with a family. When John was born, they doted on him with the attention he continues to receive to this day. Since he was a child, John has been groomed to take over my father's business. John has not yet married because I believe, he cannot find a woman who could possibly lavish him with the same attention he receives from my parents. When Peter was born, well, they already had their heir and Peter did not receive the attention he should have. Perhaps that is what drove him to self-reflection and his calling to the Church."

"What about the way *you* were treated?"

"From the time I was old enough to remember, I was told that I must marry well and raise the family's standing in the *ton*. I was never given any choice in the way I styled my hair or the clothes I wore. My mother read fashion magazines and observed all the women in Town, and I was dressed to look just like the women described in the society pages. Although I resisted their efforts to marry me to Lord Howard, I have obeyed their directives about what to do and say my entire life."

"Emily, you have been used as a pawn in your

parents' scheme to better themselves. It is unforgivable."

"Since my husband died, I have spent a great deal of time thinking about my life. I have been able to see the mistakes I made in my past and I am ready to move forward with an open mind."

"Thank you for sharing the heartache you have endured for too many years. Let us walk back to the house. I know I could use something to drink!"

SEVERAL DAYS LATER, THEY WERE OUT WALKING IN Rosings' gardens and he led her away from the topiaries. They soon reached a large field of wildflowers in full bloom. "It is so beautiful here. The colors are breathtaking!"

"My aunt worked for many years to tame and sculpt all the trees and shrubs near the house and I do not wish to let them grow wild. Years ago, Darcy and I found this field of wildflowers and it became our favorite spot on the estate. I knew I had to bring you here."

"Thank you for sharing this special place with me."

He took her hand and kissed it before going down on one knee. He grimaced from the pain of being in that position, but he wanted to tell her what was in his heart despite any temporary discomfort. "Emily, since the night of the Harvest Ball at Pemberley, I knew I wanted you in my life. I was walking toward the terrace for some fresh air when I heard a child crying. When I looked around, I saw you comforting a little boy. I believe my heart was yours from that moment on. These past days with you have been the happiest of my life. You are everything I have dreamed about when I thought about being married. I dream about you and sharing my life with you every night. You are beautiful and kind and we share so many interests. You make me so happy and I love you as I never thought I could love anyone. Please do me the great honor of accepting my hand in marriage."

"Richard, please stand up, I can see you are in pain." He slowly rose to his feet while holding her hand. She put her other hand on his, "thank you for your beautiful proposal. I am honored by your words, but I cannot give you my answer today. I want to be sure of my feelings, please give me more time to be sure."

Richard was disappointed with her response but felt in his heart that she loved him. He understood that she was afraid to marry again unless she was quite sure of her feelings. He smiled at Emily and kissed her hand again as they slowly walked back to Rosings.

CHAPTER 20

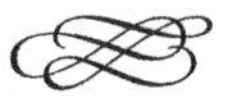

Several days later, Richard and Emily were out riding and he thought about what he could do to make her look at him as a man she could love. "Emily, do you think I can jump over that hedge?"

"Yes, I am sure you can, but it is foolhardy to try. I am not an innocent young girl you need to impress." Shortly after her words left her lips, he took off and rode rapidly toward the hedge. The next few minutes were a blur; Richard flying through the air and Emily finding him lying motionless on the ground. She was relieved to see that he was still breathing and she knew her only option was to ride back to Rosings for help. She breathlessly told Mrs. Elkins to call for the doctor and to find some men to follow her and bring Richard back to the house. Lady Emily led the rescue party to where Richard was lying motionless on the ground and asked the men to be very gentle as they placed him on the litter they brought with them.

Moments later, the footmen lifted Richard onto his bed while he was still unconscious. Emily looked at his motionless body and began crying and praying for him to live. *Please wake up my darling Richard! I love you, how very much I love you.*

The doctor arrived shortly after Richard was brought back to the house. When he finished his examination, he left his patient to speak with Mrs. Elkins about the care Richard would need. As he walked toward the stairs, he saw Lady Emily pacing back and forth in the hallway. "Lady Howard, I thought I would find you downstairs in the drawing room."

"Please, Mr. Benson, how is Mr. Fitzwilliam?"

"I have given him a thorough examination. Somehow, he does not seem to have any broken bones, but he does have a significant bump on his head. For the time being, there is very little that can be done for him until he awakens."

"Do you believe that he will wake up? Please, sir, you must tell me the truth," Lady Emily asked with tears in her eyes.

"What he needs more than anything else is time to heal. I can see that his health is very important to you and I will ask you and the rest of the staff to let him rest. You must try to get him to drink – water, tea, broth – as much as you can get him to swallow. When he does awaken, he will most likely have a very bad headache and I will leave some laudanum with Mrs. Elkins. Good day madam, I will see you tomorrow morning but please send word if he awakens or seems to be in distress."

"I thank you for your care and for coming so quickly. I will see you in the morning." When Lady Emily tried to enter Richard's chambers, she found the door was locked. She knocked softly and after a few minutes Barton opened the door a few inches. "I would like to see Mr. Fitzwilliam."

"I am trying to get him cleaned up and out of his clothes. Not an easy task without his cooperation. I will send one of the maids to summon you when he is presentable."

"Thank you, Barton, I will be in my sitting room whenever you wish to send word."

"Yes, my Lady."

Mrs. Elkins was waiting downstairs for the doctor to give her instructions. When he saw her, he handed her a small bottle of laudanum. "If Mr. Fitzwilliam awakens enough to complain about a headache, mix a few drops into a cup of tea and that should help relieve the pain and allow him to sleep."

"Is there anything else I can do?"

"He needs to rest. He has had a severe trauma to his

head, and he needs to heal. He may wake up as soon as tomorrow or it could be longer. He should be afforded quiet and care and our prayers. I have seen many a man after they had fallen off a horse. When they land on their heads, each case has been different; some wake up after a few hours and some, I am sorry to say, *never* wake up."

"Oh, no, he must get better! I have known him since he was just a boy visiting his Aunt Catherine with Lord and Lady Matlock. Should we send word to his parents?"

"Let us wait a few days and see how his recovery progresses. There is always time to share bad news."

"Did you speak to Lady Howard yet?"

"Yes, I told her exactly what I told you." The doctor paused and thought about what he was about to say. He had known Mrs. Elkins for more than twenty years and was comfortable telling her, "I believe she is quite in love with him."

"I believe you are correct and from what I have seen, the feeling is mutual. I will pray that he will heal quickly. I believe if he does, we will be hearing about a wedding in the near future."

"I concur, she is more concerned about him than a family friend would be. I will return in the morning to examine Mr. Fitzwilliam but please send word if I am needed before then."

"Thank you, Mr. Benson, I will see you to your carriage."

EMILY SPENT A SLEEPLESS NIGHT WORRYING ABOUT Richard and very early the following morning, she quietly entered his bed chamber. Barton had slept in a chair near the bed and when she entered the room, Barton awoke. "Has there been any change?"

"No, my Lady, he has not moved since yesterday."

"Barton, please break your fast and rest, I will stay with him now. I will call for you if he stirs."

"Thank you, madam, I will return in an hour." Barton bowed to her before leaving the room. He knew an unmarried woman should not be alone with a man in his bed chamber; he also knew that the nobility behaved anyway they wanted. *It is not my duty to remind her of the lack of propriety. There is little chance of anything improper happening while my master is unconscious.*

Lady Emily took the chair which Barton had vacated and moved it closer to the bed. When she sat down, she took Richard's hand and pressed it to her heart. "Please, Richard, you must wake up." Tears began to fall from her eyes and fell on their joined hands. "I cannot lose you, my love. I know I love you. I love you with all of my heart. I am sorry it took your riding accident for me to realize what you mean to me. Wake up, my dearest man so I can tell you how I feel and how much I desire to be your wife. I long to tell you how much I long to comfort our own child in my arms. Please, dear God, please bring him back to me."

Richard began to groan and brought Emily's hand to his lips without opening his eyes. He tried to move his body, but he quickly placed his hand on his head where most of the pain was. When he opened his eyes, a tearful Emily was sitting at his bedside. Richard said in a groggy voice, "was I dreaming, or did I just hear you confess your love for me and accept my proposal?"

"Yes," Emily laughed through her tears, "you foolish man, you heard me. I love you and I will happily marry you, but if you ever again try to do anything stupid to win my favor, I will never speak to you."

He brought her hand to his lips again and spoke slowly. "It seems to me that falling on my head, while I assure you was completely unintentional, has served me very well. We will be happy, Emily, that I promise you." He looked into his beloved's eyes and smiled. "Let us marry as quickly as possible. Now that you have agreed, I am anxious to make you my wife." When he attempted to sit up, he quickly laid back on his pillow. "My head feels like my horse stepped on it, several times. How long until I am well enough to carry you off to Gretna Green?"

"The doctor left some laudanum with Mrs. Elkins. A little of it in a cup of tea should help your pain. Are you hurt anywhere else? Mr. Benson examined you but did not believe that you had broken any bones, only your head injury and some bumps and bruises."

"I am happy to hear that, as you well know, I have a very thick scull and would not accept 'no' for an answer from you."

"I am happy you persisted, although I am as anxious to wed as you are, I think we should focus on your recovery for now. My parents will not be happy about me marrying you, you being a *second* son and all." Richard smiled at his beloved fiancée's teasing words. "The last thing we need to do is elope; that would make our marriage twice as hard for them to accept. After you have been restored to health, why do we not travel north together to Suffolk and tell my parents our good news. From there we can continue on to Matlock and inform your family. When we get to Pemberley for the Harvest Ball, we can tell Peter and the Darcys. My brother is one family member I believe will welcome our news."

"I can try to forgive your parents for forcing you to marry Howard; I do hope to begin our married life on good terms with your family. We are old enough and financially independent enough to make our own decisions and our own happiness. Now, will you please summon Barton, I need some help getting cleaned up and changing my clothes. I will see you shortly, my love."

"I like hearing you call me that." She leaned over and

briefly kissed him on the lips. "We are betrothed, after all," she said coquettishly and left the room.

Happiness is mine at last! Now I need to get rid of this feeling that a cow is sitting on my head, so I can kiss my fiancée properly! Richard's valet soon entered the room and helped him with his ablutions.

AFTER WAKING UP, RICHARD MADE SLOW BUT STEADY progress in his recovery. Day by day, his headache diminished, and he spent more and more time out of bed. Finally, the day arrived when Mr. Benson declared him fully healed. After his final examination, the doctor asked Barton to bring Lady Howard into Richard's chambers. When she arrived, Richard was dressed and sitting in a chair. She stood beside him and Mr. Benson said, "may I offer my heartiest congratulations on your betrothal; I am delighted for you both. I am also happy to tell you that your fiancé is fully recovered. However, I do not advise him to jump over any hedges in the future."

"Thank you so much for your excellent care," she said as she smiled at her fiancé. "I will make sure that he does not try anything that might be dangerous."

"I am delighted that I am better but I wonder if Mr. Benson has any special potions in his medical bag. Something that will make your parents accept our betrothal without me incurring another head injury!"

Everyone laughed at his joke but they were both anxious about the Carters' reaction to their news.

"Lady Howard, I have known the Fitzwilliam family for many, many years. I got to know them all during their frequent visits to Rosings to see Lady Catherine and her daughter. They are a very fine family and I cannot imagine any reason for Lord and Lady Matlock to object to you joining their family."

"I thank you for your reassurances. It is not the Fitzwilliams we worry about, but *my* family. You have never met my mother but if you had, you would understand our anxiety. However, we are adults and we will not be dissuaded from marrying by anyone or anything." He took her hand and placed a kiss on it before smiling at the determined words of the woman he loved.

"Well, I have done all I can do. Mr. Fitzwilliam, I would like to remind you to desist from jumping over anything higher than a blade of grass. I wish you both every happiness."

"Thank you for your care, Mr. Benson. Barton, please escort the doctor to his carriage." Richard waited until they were alone before he pulled Emily onto his lap and passionately kissed her.

When their kiss ended, Emily rested her head on his shoulder, and he heard her whisper, "I never knew a kiss could feel like that."

"My darling Emily, you have never been kissed by a man you love and who loves you in return. You have no idea what passion lies ahead of us. On our wedding night, it will be as if it were your first time, because it *will* be your first time with the man you love."

"I could not agree with you more and the sooner we wed the better. I am anxious to begin our life together."

"Rosings brings in about five thousand a year. I have a small inheritance from my grandmother and some other investments that Darcy advised me on when I sold my commission. I have no idea what your finances are, nor do I care. We will certainly be able to live well on my income."

"I have a great deal of money of my own. The truth is that my husband died before he could spend too much of it. Much of my marriage settlement and a portion of my dowry are under my control. So, it appears that you are betrothed to an independently wealthy woman," Emily teased.

"Just as long as you are my wife, I care not if you have a farthing on our wedding day." He briefly kissed her and smiled. "When shall we leave for Suffolk? Is two days' time enough for you to prepare? I will speak to my steward today about the upcoming harvest and our plans to be away for a time."

"I will send an express to my parents letting them know our arrival date and I will start packing now!"

Richard did not release his fiancée from his embrace. "I will make all the arrangements for our travel. I plan to reserve two separate rooms for us. Your maid and Barton will also travel with us and we will observe all the dictates of society. I will not have anyone questioning the propriety of our trip or malign our relationship."

"Thank you, I was hoping you would say that. I believe we should tell everyone that we met by chance in Kent. I assume we can depend on your staff's discretion. No reason for anyone to know that I have stayed with you in your home for several weeks."

"Madam, once again, you have come up with a perfect plan."

"Now, let me up! I really must start my packing!"

"Not so fast, my lady. I believe your newly recovered fiancé needs another kiss."

"I am delighted to give you anything you need, my dearest man," she said as she tenderly caressed his face.

THAT NIGHT, LONG AFTER HE HAD BID EMILY GOOD night, Richard was pacing in his chambers when he got an idea. He knew the rest of the house was asleep as he quietly made his way to Emily's bed chamber. He put his ear to her door and heard his fiancée singing quietly. He gently knocked and the door was quickly opened. "Richard, what are you doing here? Are you unwell?"

"I just felt the need to see you one more time before I go to bed. I hope I have not disturbed you but I heard you singing and knew you must be awake."

She placed her hand on his arm, "I always sing when I am happy, and tonight I am particularly joyous."

"In that case, do you think your poor lonely fiancé could have a good night kiss?"

"I think that may be arranged," she said as she walked even closer and kissed the man she had come to love so much. He did not stay long and as he walked back to his chambers, he found he was also singing!

CHAPTER 21

The next morning, Emily sent an express to her parents announcing her return to Ipswich. She told them there was no need for them to send the Carter carriage back to Kent; she would be traveling with her friend. They stopped for the night at an inn along the way and planned to arrive at the Carter's estate in the early afternoon. Emily took Richard's arm as they entered the house and she led them to the drawing room. When her parents looked up and saw their daughter arm in arm with Richard, her father found his voice first. "What is the meaning of this? Take your hand off that man!" Richard heard the venom in his voice and was happy he was taking Emily away from these small minded social-climbers.

"No father, I shall not remove my hand from the arm of the man I love and will soon marry. Yes, mother, I can see by your expression that you are in shock.

Richard and I love each other and will be very happy together. I am old enough and financially secure enough to make my own decisions. I will not allow you to trap me into another farce of a marriage. For the first time in a long while, I am truly happy. I will only marry again for love and as soon as possible, Richard Fitzwilliam will be my husband."

"Emily, how can you throw away the opportunity to be the wife of a peer, a man of wealth and a title?"

"Mother, I am not throwing anything away. I am a good daughter and obediently followed your demands and married Lord Howard. Now, I am going to follow my heart. Richard owns a large estate in Kent and his father is a peer." Emily paused and took a few steps toward her parents. "We would like to stay here for a few days before traveling to Derbyshire where we will share our good news with Lord and Lady Matlock."

"I am sure Lady Matlock, will be in touch with you as soon as she knows of our betrothal. We are willing to have the wedding in London, if that is what you prefer. I hope you will give us your blessing for we *will* marry as soon as possible."

Tension enveloped the room as Richard and Emily nervously awaited her parents' reaction to their news. After several long minutes, her father stood and walked toward them. "I suppose we have no other choice but to congratulate you both and wish you every joy in your marriage."

"Thank you, Papa, we appreciate your kind words." Mr. Carter shook Richard's hand and they all turned toward Mrs. Carter awaiting her approval. She was staring straight ahead and would not look at Emily and Richard. They all waited a few moments before Emily asked her father, "may I instruct the housekeeper to prepare a guest suite for Richard?"

Her mother jumped to her feet. "No, you will not! I will take care of it. I am the mistress of this house!"

"Mrs. Carter, I hope we can get to know each other over the next few days. I realize you are surprised by our news, but I assure you, we will be married, with or without your blessing."

"We will see about that!" She stormed out of the room and began shouting for the housekeeper.

"I was hoping Mama would see how happy I am. I love Richard and we will marry as quickly as possible, but I was hoping to have the blessing of both my parents."

"Give your mother some time, Emily, you know she had other plans for you. She only wants you to maintain your standing in the *ton*. As you said, you certainly do not need our permission to marry."

"I wish both my parents could share in my joy, but Richard and I are prepared to move forward without it. Mama should consider the fact that by this time next year, I may be with child, your first grandchild. I would like our children to enjoy the affections of all four grandparents. I will retire to my room now and meet you for dinner. Richard, I will send someone to escort you to your room." Emily kissed her father's cheek and then turned and quickly kissed Richard before leaving the drawing room.

There were several more awkward minutes when Mr. Carter and Richard were alone in the drawing room. Mr. Carter asked how they met, and Richard told him of meeting her for the first time in Derbyshire. He told him about their walks together after the Townsend's Ball and meeting Emily in Kent while she was visiting Lady Mary Greenley. "We would have been here sooner, but I fell off my horse and landed on my head. I was unconscious for a time and took some time to heal." Richard told him more about his accident and how Emily came to realize her true feelings for him.

"I suppose you look well enough now."

"I was hoping to meet your son John before we travel to Matlock."

"John is away with some friends. I do not know when he will return to Suffolk." Mr. Carter said brusquely. He noticed a footman in the doorway, "here is Rhodes to show you to your room. I will see you for dinner." Mr. Carter did not look at him as he walked past Richard as he left the drawing room.

. . .

THE REMAINDER OF THEIR DAYS IN SUFFOLK WERE MUCH the same. Mr. Carter was guarded in his interactions with Richard and Mrs. Carter did not speak or look at Richard or her daughter. Emily and Richard walked in the gardens and took a few excursions into Ipswich. On the morning of their departure for Derbyshire, Mr. Carter stood near the front door with the happy couple; he shook Richard's hand and kissed Emily's cheek. When they began to leave the house, everyone turned when they heard Mrs. Carter shouting, "wait, wait for me!" When she reached them, she was breathing quickly and crying. "Emily, please forgive me. I love you and only want you to be happy. If Mr. Fitzwilliam is the man you love and believe you will be happy with, you have my blessing. Can you ever forgive my behavior?"

She embraced her weeping mother, "Mama, of course I forgive you; I am so happy, and I love Richard. Let us start over from the time we arrived here. Mother, allow me to present my fiancé, Richard Fitzwilliam. Richard, I am happy to introduce my mother."

Richard took Mrs. Carter's hand and bowed over it. "It is a pleasure to meet you, Mrs. Carter." He turned to Emily, "perhaps we can delay our departure until tomorrow. I am certain you and your mother have many things to discuss in regard to planning our wedding. I will send an express to my parents telling them of my new arrival date." Richard turned to Emily's parents. "They have no idea that I will be accompanied by Lady Howard."

"Thank you, my dear. I would love to have some time with my mother; we must discuss wedding dates, dresses, flowers, ribbons and lace. And many other topics of which I am sure you and Papa have no interest."

"Richard, why do we not leave the ladies to their discussion of fripperies and relax in my study with some brandy and the newspaper?"

"Mr. Carter, that sounds like a wonderful idea!"

The following day, they departed from Derbyshire but not before everyone kissed, shook hands, embraced and spoke about reuniting as soon as possible. Mrs. Carter and Emily cried and continued to embrace each other as they stood near the carriage door. Richard helped Emily into the vehicle and turned to Mrs. Carter and bowed to her.

She walked toward him and said through her tears, "farewell, Richard. Travel safely and give my best wishes to Lord and Lady Matlock." She then stood on her tiptoes and kissed his cheek.

"Madam, I will be delighted to convey your good wishes." He would never know what prompted Mrs. Carter's sudden change of heart but was grateful that Emily was elated to receive the blessings of both her parents.

AS THE CARRIAGE PULLED AWAY AND THEY ENTERED THE

main road, Richard looked at his tearful fiancée, "My love, what is it? Are you well?"

"I am happy, that is all." Emily looked down at her tear-soaked handkerchief, "when my parents forced me to marry Howard, they disregarded my wishes and my pleas to stop the marriage from taking place. I was miserable after the wedding and was almost always alone; I convinced myself that my parents behaved as they did because they did not love me. Now I know that it is not true; they may not have shown me their love as I would have liked, but I do know they love me. Do you know what my mother told me? She said the reason they threw Lord Hedley out of the house was not just because he had no money, but because he reminded them both too much of Lord Howard. So, I suppose that is how they demonstrated their love for me."

"How could anyone not love you? You are the most wonderful woman in England."

"Thank you, my love, but I feel your observations are not, in any way, objective."

"During your stay at Rosings, I saw you taking note of the draperies, fabrics and rugs. I want you to redecorate the house to suit your tastes. Most of what is there is the handiwork of my Aunt Catherine who preferred anything ornate that was embellished with gold. I never felt the need to change anything until now. The house should reflect your tastes and the sooner the better."

"Thank you, my love, I already have several changes in mind." They both laughed and settled into the carriage they would occupy for the next few days.

~

AT BIRCHWOOD MANOR, CAROLINE WAS PLAYING A game on the back lawn with Maddie. They were trying to roll a ball into a toppled wooden bucket; the farther their attempts were from reaching their goal, the more they both laughed. Caroline was so involved with entertaining her niece, it took her several minutes to notice that Peter Carter was standing near the trees and watching them. "Mr. Carter, I am surprised to see you. I hope you have not been standing there long enough to observe my poor aim."

"On the contrary, Miss Bingley, I have been observing a scene of pure delight." She blushed, and Maddie's nanny took her charge indoors for a rest. "Perhaps, if you are not too tired, we can walk together in the garden?"

"I would like that very much." She took his arm and they walked in silence for several minutes.

"I know I asked you for a courtship when we were together at the Bingley's Ball."

"Yes, and I told you that if my past behavior was an impediment to your happiness, I would not hold you to our courtship." She was on the verge of tears and her stomach was in knots. She feared that her behavior before she met Peter would mean the end of her relationship with the only man she had ever loved. She held her breath dreading what he would say next.

He stopped walking and took both of her hands in his. "When will you realize that I love you? I care not what you were like before we met. I love you for who you are; the lovely young woman who helps me in my parish, the caring sister and aunt you are now. Caroline, please listen to me closely." Peter got down on one knee and continued, "I want you to be my wife. I want you by my side always. I want to look outside the rectory and see you playing ball with our children. I want you in my bed every night, perhaps a man of the cloth should not speak that way, but I am still a man. A man desperately in love with a beautiful, caring and kind woman. Please end my suffering and tell me you will be my wife. Caroline Angela Bingley, will you marry me?"

"Please stand up you silly man. How can you have any doubt? I have been in love with you since we danced together at the Harvest Ball. Yes, Peter, a hundred times, yes. I will marry you and I long to be your wife." Peter embraced his betrothed and timidly touched his lips to hers. She responded by placing her hand on his face and they enjoyed a less tentative kiss.

"I believe the best course of action is for us to go inside. I am sure you wish to tell Mr. and Mrs. Bingley our happy news."

"Yes, Jane will be relieved; I have been speaking to her about you for months and months. She and Charles will be delighted that I have made a love match, but would you mind if we did not tell anyone just yet. I would like us to enjoy the knowledge of our love and commitment before we share our news."

"I will do as you wish. There *is* something special about us being the only ones to know our wonderful news."

They walked arm in arm toward the house when Caroline stopped and looked at her fiancé. "Thank you, Peter. Thank you for loving me and wanting me as your wife. I never thought I could be this happy. Thank you, my dearest man."

He took her hand and kissed it over and over again. "Please do not thank me again for loving you. You are the woman I have waited for my whole life and being with you has brought me so much joy. No more talk of thanks, I believe it is time for a cup of tea!"

CHAPTER 22

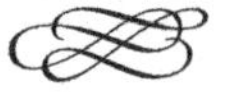

SEPTEMBER 1814

After three long days of traveling, Richard and Emily reached Matlock Manor. They were shown into the drawing room but Richard asked Emily to stand out of sight until he was ready to introduce her. "Good day, Mama, Papa, I am happy to see you. I hope you do not mind that I brought someone with me."

Both his parents rose to greet him. "Richard, it is so good to see you! Did you bring a friend? One of your army associates?" Lady Matlock asked as she walked toward her son and embraced him.

"I think you will be happy to see who I have brought with me and it is not one of my army friends." Richard left the drawing room and walked back in with Emily on his arm. "Mama, Papa, pray allow me the honor of presenting my fiancée, Lady Emily Howard."

"What a lovely surprise! Welcome to Matlock, Lady Howard. We are so happy to see you again."

"Thank you, my lady, but I beg you to call me Emily or Lady Emily, if you must. After we are married, I will be very happy to be known as Mrs. Emily Fitzwilliam."

Lady Matlock embraced Emily and her husband bowed before her and kissed her hand. She was escorted to a nearby settee and her future mother in law sat beside her. "I knew my mother would completely ignore me and take my beloved Emily from my side." They all laughed at Richard's tease.

"We are happily astonished by the news. We had no idea you and Richard were seeing each other."

"We met about a year ago at the Darcy's Harvest Ball. Following my husband's death, I went to Derbyshire to spend some time with my brother, Peter, and act as his hostess at the rectory. I believe you met him when you were guests at Pemberley for Christmastide. Richard and I saw each other many times at Pemberley and then again, this past winter in London. I will let Richard tell you the rest of our story."

"There is not much more to tell. Emily came to Kent to visit a friend and we ran into each other at a lawn party and I pursued her to the best of my ability. I was determined to make Emily my wife and knew I had to do everything in my power to win her hand.

However, in an attempt to impress her, I tried to jump over a hedge and fell off my horse and landed on my head!"

"You foolish man! What were you thinking? Are you well? Sakes alive, all men are just large boys," Lady Matlock rolled her eyes at Emily with feigned disgust.

"I am fine, Mama, I was knocked out for a day, but my accident led Emily to reveal her love for me and her acceptance of my proposal. We have already traveled to Suffolk to tell Emily's parents our good news and then we came here. We would like to spend some time with you, so you can get to know Emily better before we travel to Pemberley for their Harvest Ball."

"Well, my dear, we have many plans to make. Have you picked a date? Will you marry in Town or at your parents' parish? We must start shopping for your trousseau as soon as possible. I will make appointments at my modiste, she always has the most beautiful fabrics and designs."

"Papa, I believe that is our cue to leave the ladies to their own devices."

"Hugh, please tell Mrs. Shields to make sure a guest suite is prepared. And please make sure her maid is shown to Lady Emily's suite, so she can begin unpacking."

Lord Matlock bowed to his wife, "Whatever you wish, m'lady," he teased as he and his son exited the room.

Once they were alone, Lady Matlock looked at her future daughter and said, "I am truly elated that you and Richard will wed. For years, he has rebuffed all my efforts at matchmaking and he seems to have known all along whom he wished to marry. Have you decided when and where you will wed?"

"We would like to be married in London, well, that is my mother's wish. We hope to marry in October as we are both anxious to begin our married life." Emily blushed at her last comment.

"Yes, my dear, I understand. Of course, the wedding breakfast will be held at Matlock House. Now, let us discuss your dress, the flowers…."

"Before we start planning for the wedding, I would like to tell you something."

"You can tell me anything you want. You will soon be my daughter!"

Emily recounted the story of how she met and was pressured into marrying Lord Howard. "I was desperately unhappy and was left alone most of the time. He only married me for my dowry and to produce an heir. What I am trying to say is that I love Richard with my whole heart; I feel as if our marriage will truly be my first. Shortly after Richard proposed, he had his accident and I feared I would never get the chance to marry your wonderful son. I thought you should know the truth."

"I thank you for your candor, Emily. There were so many rumors floating around the *ton,* I am glad I now know the truth. I watched my son's face since you arrived here, and I can see how he looks at you. It is easy to see how much he loves you. I never thought Richard would marry and now, I could not be happier for you both." Lady Matlock put her arms around her future daughter and embraced her. "Welcome to the family, my dear, I am sure you will both be very happy."

They spent a few days with Richard's parents and when they departed Lady Matlock assured her Emily that she would write to her at Pemberley. She would let Emily know when she was expected in London to visit the modiste and acquire everything else she would need before her marriage. They were all joyful when the betrothed couple departed to join the Darcys for their Harvest Ball. Emily was most anxious to see her brother and share their happy news with Peter as well as the Darcys. She sent a letter to her brother telling him of her visit to Derbyshire and informing him that she would be staying at Pemberley. She did not wish to disrupt his schedule by staying at the rectory, but she assured him of a visit shortly after she arrived.

~

When Richard's carriage stopped in front of Pemberley's entrance, the Darcys stepped outside to welcome him. When he turned to help Emily out, Darcy and Elizabeth smiled as they looked at each other with many unspoken questions. "Welcome, Richard! Lady Emily, what a pleasant surprise. We are delighted to have you join us."

"Thank you for your warm welcome, Mrs. Darcy. I had hoped that Mr. Fitzwilliam would have told you that I would be accompanying him."

"I did tell Darcy. If he has forgotten to inform his wife, I cannot take the blame!" They all laughed at Richard's teasing. "I wrote to Darcy and explained that Lady Emily was traveling with me and would like to stay at Pemberley so as not to interfere with her brother's responsibilities."

Darcy looked embarrassed and said, "This is all my fault and I apologize for any awkwardness. I did receive Richard's letter, but I was busy with too many things and confess I only read the first part of his letter apprising me of his arrival date. I am sure Mrs. Reynolds can make whatever arrangements are necessary for Lady Emily's stay with us."

"Thank you, Mr. Darcy, I am sorry for the inconvenience."

"No inconvenience I assure you, please, let us all go in. Georgiana has been eagerly awaiting her cousin's arrival."

Elizabeth spoke to Mrs. Reynolds as soon as they entered the house. A few minutes later the housekeeper entered the drawing room where the Darcys and their guests had gathered. "Lady Howard, your rooms are ready if you would like to refresh yourself after your trip. Your maid is already there unpacking your trunks."

"Thank you, Mrs. Reynolds. If you will excuse me, I will see you all for dinner." Emily smiled to the room and tried not to look at her fiancé but her love for Richard overpowered her restraint. Anyone who was watching saw her looking at him adoringly before turning to depart the room.

Before anyone had a chance to ask Richard what was going on between him and Lady Emily, a footman entered the room. He announced that the Bingley's carriage was nearing the house and Darcy, Elizabeth and Georgiana left the room to greet their guests. Richard took advantage of being alone and quickly walked up the stairs and entered his usual guest room. He knew he had only delayed Darcy bombarding him with questions regarding Lady Emily.

~

WHILE EVERYONE WAS RESTING BEFORE DINNER, Richard and Emily traveled to Kympton to see her brother. They were surprised to see that Caroline Bingley was there having tea with the vicar. Peter was very happy to see the glow on his sister's face and was delighted when she told him that she and Richard were engaged to be married. Peter looked at Caroline for her approval of announcing their betrothal to his sister and her fiancé. She nodded and came to stand beside him while he announced, "I am so happy for you, Emily, and you, Mr. Fitzwilliam. I also have some news, I have asked Miss Bingley for her hand in marriage and she has accepted!" Words of congratulations and best wishes were expressed by all and everyone was happy.

Caroline stood beside her fiancé and looked at their guests. "Please call me Caroline, both of you. Lady Howard, I must tell you how happy I am to be marrying your brother and to having you as my sister. I suppose I will have to get used to having you, Mr. Fitzwilliam, as a brother!" They all laughed before Richard asked Caroline and Peter to call him by his Christian name.

"And please, no more of this Lady anything, I would be very happy if you called me Emily." Emily and Caroline embraced while Richard and Peter shook hands.

"Caroline and I wish to be married here in Kympton. Mr. Hatcher, the former vicar has agreed to officiate."

"Peter, you will not be surprised that Mama wishes me to marry in Town and Lady Matlock insisted on hosting the wedding breakfast."

"As long as we are married, I do not care where we are," Richard added as he smiled at his betrothed. "Have you told anyone about your betrothal yet?"

"No, the Bingleys and I have been invited to dine at Pemberley this evening and we thought we would tell everyone at that time."

"Peter, that sounds like a fine plan. We will let you and Caroline make your announcement first and let you enjoy your moment. After that, Emily and I will make our news known to all. We must return to Pemberley now. We shall see you both at dinner."

After the guests had departed, Peter approached his fiancée. "While we were all congratulating each other, I got an idea. What do you think about Emily and Richard sharing our wedding day? I know Emily would like nothing more than a small quiet affair. Her wedding to Lord Howard was like watching a badly staged production with an unhappy bride."

"I think it is a wonderful idea. Shall we ask how they feel about it this evening?"

"Yes, no time like the present!

As soon as they entered the carriage, Emily asked, "why did Caroline say it would be difficult getting used to calling you Richard?"

"Charles Bingley is one of Darcy's closest friends.

Over the years, I have frequently been in his company as well as both his sisters. The woman who is betrothed to your brother is not the same woman I have spent time within the past. She used to be the most mean-spirited, social climbing harpy. She set her cap on Darcy as soon as Charles introduced them. While they were in Hertfordshire, she always spoke very poorly of Elizabeth. I suppose she thought that criticizing everything about the object of Darcy's affection would raise her up in Darcy's eyes. Darcy never gave Caroline any indication that he was interested in her in any way.

"There was no love on her part either, she was only interested in his wealth and connections to the *ton*. Obviously, she has undergone some kind of transformation. The woman I saw today was happy, kind and welcoming. Meeting your brother must have made her realize the kind of person she truly wants to be. I hope they will be very happy together."

"As do I, my love. I can tell you that I have never seen Peter look happier and we should accept Caroline for the person she is now."

"Yes, my dear, I agree."

CHAPTER 23

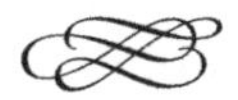

That evening, Darcy entered Elizabeth's chambers just as her maid was closing the clasp on his wife's pearl necklace. "Thank you, Hannah, that will be all. I will ring when I need you later."

"Yes, Mrs. Darcy, sir," her maid curtsied to them both and left the room.

"I know that look on your face. You want to talk about Richard and Lady Emily." Elizabeth rose from her dressing table and walked across her room to sit on the settee. She patted the cushion beside her; inviting her husband to join her.

"I have known Richard my entire life," he said as he sat down. "He has never kept any secrets from me. Do you think they are already married, or betrothed? He spoke to us both about his feelings months ago in London. Perhaps, they are having an affair. I believe my feelings are a bit hurt by my cousin's surprising lack of information."

"My love, I feel we will know the nature of their relationship in the very near future. I strongly doubt that they are having an affair. Lady Emily would never flaunt her lover in front of her brother. He is a man of God, after all, and Lady Emily would never humiliate him. Why do we not meet our guests in the drawing room and perhaps learn more there?"

"I know you are correct, Richard is the most honorable man I know. He would never bring his lover to our home, especially not with Georgiana living here."

A FEW MINUTES LATER THEY JOINED EVERYONE WHO WAS gathered in the drawing room; Jane, Charles and Georgiana were sitting together. Caroline, Richard, and Peter and Emily were standing together, a good distance from the other guests. Peter said quietly to his sister, "we would like to invite you and Richard to marry here in Derbyshire and share our wedding day."

Richard and Emily looked at each other and smiled; neither of them wanted a big society wedding in London. Marrying alongside Peter and Caroline sounded like a perfect way to avoid all the trappings that Lady Matlock and Mrs. Carter would plan. "Lady Emily and I would be delighted to join you at the altar. We will have to apprise our parents of this change of venue as soon as possible. I suppose we should pick a specific date, so we can announce everything at once," Richard said.

"Caroline and I were thinking about the twenty fifth of October. That would give you ladies six weeks to take care of all the things new brides need taking care of!" They all nodded their heads in agreement.

"Peter, Richard and I are as anxious to wed as you and Caroline." They all smiled as they rejoined the others.

WHEN ALL THE GUESTS WERE ASSEMBLED AND EVERYONE was enjoying a glass of wine, Darcy stood by the mantel and asked for everyone's attention. "Elizabeth, Georgiana and I are very happy to have you all here for the Harvest Ball. You were all with us one year ago, the year we brought the Harvest Ball back to Pemberley. Our little Bennet was not yet born and soon we will celebrate his first birthday. We welcome you all and wish everyone good health!" Everyone raised their glasses to toast all the blessings they enjoyed.

Peter began to speak as soon as the toast was over, "Excuse the intrusion everyone, but I have some very good news to share with my family and friends." They all looked around the room and no one could imagine the words that came next. "I am delighted to announce that Miss Caroline Bingley and I are engaged to be married!" Peter reached out his hand and Caroline walked across the room to take it. Jane was the only one in the room who was not surprised by the announcement and everyone expressed their happiness to the newly betrothed couple. Caroline had spoken to Jane of her feelings many times and although Jane shared their sister's feelings with her husband, it seemed that Charles did not take his wife's words seriously. Charles was thrilled for his sister but still surprised that she allowed herself to marry for love and not a title or great wealth. He had to admit that he had *never* seen Caroline look so happy.

After all the congratulations were over, Richard asked for everyone's attention and said, "I, too, would like to share some good news." Everyone looked at Richard with amazement; he had been a bachelor for so long, no one believed he could possibly be announcing *his* betrothal. "I am absolutely delighted to tell you that my days as an unmarried man are soon over. Next month, Lady Emily and I will also wed, and we could not be happier!" Richard walked to Emily's side and kissed her hand. Elizabeth, Georgiana and Darcy were delighted for their cousin and there were many more kisses and embraces.

The discussion before dinner was centered on the two newly engaged couples. When Richard told everyone the date of the wedding and that they would share the date with Peter and Caroline, everyone thought it was a splendid idea.

"Elizabeth and I would like to host the wedding breakfast here at Pemberley," Darcy said. He looked at his wife and she smiled at him in agreement with his suggestion. Richard looked at his cousin and the two men smiled and nodded at each other with brotherly love.

"Mr. Carter, since you are the vicar at Kympton, who will officiate at the wedding?" Georgiana asked, and everyone looked at Peter for his response.

"Miss Darcy, that is a very good question. I have asked Mr. Hatcher to briefly come out of retirement to perform the ceremony and he told me that he would be very happy to do so."

Darcy stood and said, "It appears that we will have two weddings next month and I am sure all the ladies in the room will have much to do to prepare. In the meantime, I believe it is time we eat!" Everyone followed Elizabeth and Darcy into the dining room where there was another round of congratulations and many toasts to the happy couples.

When the ladies left the gentlemen to their brandy and cigars, Charles and Peter began a private conversation about Caroline and her dowry and other matters for which the head of the Bingley family was responsible. Darcy and Richard began their own private conversation, "Richard, I am very happy for you, but your announcement took us by surprise. We had no idea you and Lady Emily had seen each other after the Townsend's Ball. How is it you were traveling together and staying overnight at inns along the way? Has there been a compromise? You know you can trust me with the truth."

"No compromise, I assure you. We were traveling with Emily's maid and my valet and we all had separate rooms. Emily was so unhappy during her marriage to Lord Howard that we are behaving as if this will be her first wedding. I would never take advantage of the woman I have loved for the past year."

"Have you spent much time together? You must admit that we knew nothing about it."

"We wanted to keep our relationship private. You have met Emily's parents; if they got wind of us spending time together, I would hate to think of the things they would have done to keep us apart. As it is, when we visited the Carter's in Suffolk, her mother would not look at me for three days. Thankfully, she came to her senses before we left and I believe she is truly happy for her daughter. I do not know how she will react to us marrying in Derbyshire, but we are determined to do what is best for our own happiness."

Darcy rose and embraced his cousin, "I am very happy for you and Lady Emily and I hope you know you will both be welcome here whenever you wish."

"Darcy, I must be honest with you. I have watched the way you and Elizabeth love each other, and I have envied your happiness. I never thought I would find the right woman, but Emily is the most wonderful person I have ever met. How would you feel about standing up for me?"

"Richard, it would be my pleasure."

THE HARVEST BALL
September 1814

THE HARVEST BALL HAD BEEN SCHEDULED TO TAKE place the evening after everyone learned of the two betrothals. During the day, Elizabeth, Georgiana and Mrs. Reynolds were busy seeing to all the last-minute details before the tenants and their other guests were to arrive.

After breakfast, Peter Carter called on Caroline at Pemberley and they, along with Richard and Lady Emily, went for a leisurely walk through the beautiful gardens surrounding the manor house. They began chatting about some of the details of their wedding and discussed the specifics of a ceremony with two brides, two grooms and four attendants. After they were finished with their talk, the two couples separated. If anyone was watching from the house, they may have seen Richard stealing a kiss or two from Emily and Peter and Caroline standing very close to each other.

"BEFORE WE GREET OUR GUESTS, I WISH TO REMIND YOU of a promise you made to me last year," Elizabeth said to her husband as they walked toward the staircase.

"A promise? I do not recall promising you anything."

"When I wished to dance last year, you promised me that this year you would dance me off my feet while our beautiful boy was happily asleep in the nursery."

"Ah, yes, now I remember. You have made your point, madam, and I would never think of backing out of a promise," Darcy said with a smile as he kissed his wife lightly on the lips.

THE SECOND HARVEST BALL AT PEMBERLEY WAS A bigger success than the first one had been. All the guests enjoyed the food, the music and the lovely gift baskets the tenants received before leaving. Once again, Georgiana kept all the children happily engaged in various games. She was very surprised when she looked up and saw David Arlington walking toward her.

"Mr. Arlington, I am happy to see you although I did not know my brother and sister had invited you."

"I wrote to Darcy and told him I was hoping to be at my family's estate this month. He wrote back and said if I was nearby, I was invited to Pemberley. I hope you are not unhappy that I am here."

"Not at all, welcome to Pemberley and I hope you enjoy the party," Georgiana turned back toward the children playing. *What is HE doing here? He smiles at me, he dances with me, he talks to me, he seems to enjoy the time we spend together and then he disappears! I will not build my hopes up again. He can just dance and speak and eat with someone else. I will not allow myself to play his game, whatever it is.*

David Arlington approached Georgiana later in the evening and asked her to dance. She could not very well say 'no' and they had a very pleasant time while they were together. After their set, he walked her back to where she had been standing with her brother and sister. He did not return to Pemberley to call on Georgiana the day after the Harvest Ball; nor did she see him again for many months.

AFTER THE HARVEST BALL, PETER WROTE TO HIS parents announcing his betrothal to Miss Caroline Bingley. He, along with Emily and Richard, wrote to their parents and announced the new wedding venue and the date of the ceremony. Emily wrote to her parents that she and her brother would be married in a double ceremony and they had already begun making wedding plans. Emily and Caroline planned to travel to London to shop for their trousseaux. Both Lady Matlock and Mrs. Carter expressed their surprise at the changed location of the wedding, but both agreed to meet the future brides in Town and assist them with their shopping as quickly as it could be arranged.

On the night before the double wedding, Elizabeth found her husband pacing in their sitting room. Darcy knew he would be expected to propose a toast to Richard and Emily. He had already told Elizabeth that he was honored to do it, but he feared he might become emotional. "William, speak from your heart and the words will come. If you feel that tears of joy will be shed, everyone will understand. I doubt it will be the only time tomorrow that happy tears will be seen," his wife advised him.

"I am so happy for both of them; I had my doubts that Richard would ever lower his guard enough to fall in love."

"I am certain that many people said the same thing about you," Elizabeth teased. Darcy nodded in agreement and went to his desk to commit his thoughts to paper.

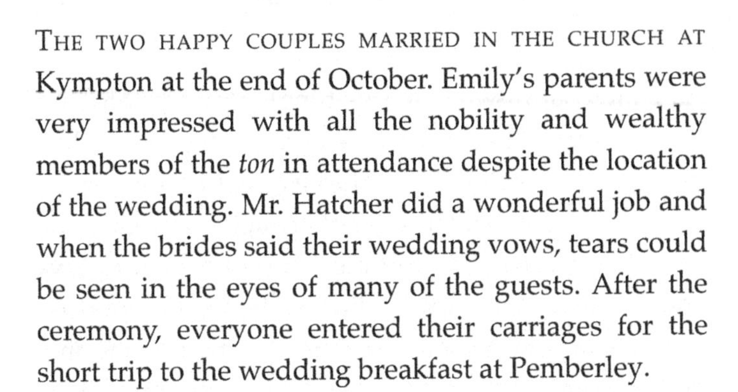

THE TWO HAPPY COUPLES MARRIED IN THE CHURCH AT Kympton at the end of October. Emily's parents were very impressed with all the nobility and wealthy members of the *ton* in attendance despite the location of the wedding. Mr. Hatcher did a wonderful job and when the brides said their wedding vows, tears could be seen in the eyes of many of the guests. After the ceremony, everyone entered their carriages for the short trip to the wedding breakfast at Pemberley.

When everyone was seated, Darcy rose to propose the toast he had been working on until the early hours. "My friends, Elizabeth, Georgiana and I are very happy to welcome you to Pemberley on this very special day." Darcy tried unsuccessfully not to look at Richard's smiling face. "I would like to be the first to propose a toast to Emily and Richard. Emily, you came into our lives last year and it has been a pleasure getting to know you better. We welcome you to the family. Richard," Darcy paused to composed himself. "Richard, I have thought of you as my brother since our childhood adventures here at Pemberley and at Matlock Manor. Those of us who know you well, had our doubts that you, as a seasoned soldier, would make yourself vulnerable enough to fall in love. However, at last year's Harvest Ball, it seems that you were instantly smitten by the lovely Lady Emily." Richard looked at his new wife and smiled before he raised her hand to his lips for a kiss. "Everyone, please, raise your glasses. Wishing our newlyweds happiness, health and love. To Emily and Richard!"

As Darcy sat down, Charles Bingley rose to propose another toast. "Last year, Jane and I watched Caroline dancing with Peter at the Harvest Ball and my sister was a changed person after that night. Caroline, we are all so happy that you have found a man to love and a new attitude toward life." Charles did not need to describe the person Caroline was before she met her husband. "We could not be happier that you have found such a loving, kind and caring man. Peter, we are very happy to welcome you to our family. Friends, please raise your glasses and toast the happy couple! To Caroline and Peter!"

Lord Matlock and Viscount Ashford also toasted Richard and Emily; Peter's father and Mr. Hurst toasted Caroline and Peter. When the toasts were over and everyone was enjoying their meal, Richard turned to his bride, "Do you think we should tell your parents that I am Mary Greenley? I worry that at some point your parents will encounter Lord and Lady Greenley in Town. I am certain they would comment on your correspondence with their daughter and your visit to their estate which is not called Rosings Park."

"They look so happy, Richard. Why spoil their enjoyment? I think that when and if we are blessed with a child, we can tell them then. I think they will be so excited for their first grandchild to arrive, that they will forgive us for all the times we have misled them."

Richard kissed his wife's hand, "I will take my direction from you, my dearest wife. Whatever you desire shall come to pass."

"Thank you, my love. Would you think I am utterly shameless if I tell you how much I am looking forward to tonight?"

Richard smiled at his wife, "no, my love, you are hardly a wanton vixen, but I am quickly losing my patience with these festivities!" The wedding breakfast was a huge success and as soon as it was acceptable, both newlywed couples left Pemberley to begin their new lives together.

Darcy had offered Peter and Caroline the use of Heatherwood, the Darcy estate in Scotland for their wedding trip. It was not too far away, and Peter was grateful for the Darcys' generosity. He did not wish to be away from his parish for an extended period of time. Mr. Hatcher graciously offered to resume the duties of vicar until the Carters returned from Scotland.

Richard and Emily traveled to Margate for their wedding trip. They rented a small seaside cottage and planned to stay for several weeks before returning to Rosings. They intended to remain in Kent until the holiday season when they had been invited to return to Pemberley for Christmastide. The Darcys had also extended an invitation to Emily and Peter's parents. They very happily accepted after they heard that Lord and Lady Matlock would also be in attendance. Darcy and Elizabeth were anxious about Mrs. Carter's reaction to Mrs. Bennet's *occasional* lack of propriety; although Lord and Lady Matlock seemed to be amused by Mrs. Bennet's lack of decorum.

By the time the Harvest Ball of 1815 took place, both Jane Bingley and Elizabeth Darcy had given birth to their second children and Emily Fitzwilliam and Caroline Carter were both happily round with child.

EPILOGUE

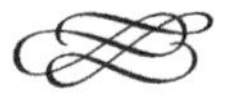

During the Season which followed the Harvest Ball of 1814, Georgiana met and danced with David Arlington at various parties in London. After one such ball, he called on her the day after they had danced together the evening before. He told her that he had never had the opportunity to call on her because he had returned to his family's estate immediately following the her ball. He explained that when they met at her coming out party, both of his parents were already quite ill and he wanted to spend as much time as possible with them. Georgiana expressed her condolences and now understood why he never called on her the day after any of their dances. After his first call at Darcy House, one visit led to another and after they spent a great deal of time together, David asked Georgiana for her hand. She could hardly say *no* to the one young man she had started to fall in love with at her coming out ball.

David was the second son of the late Duke and Duchess Hamilton of Hilltop Manor, a large estate that was less than 10 miles from Pemberley. Darcy was familiar with David's family and after a short deliberation (not to mention vigorous urging from Elizabeth and Georgiana), he finally gave his blessing for his beloved sister to marry. Georgiana and David married from Pemberley and shortly before their first wedding anniversary, Georgiana gave birth to their daughter, Beth Anne. It was not long after his daughter's birth that David's older brother was tragically killed in a riding accident. Georgiana was now a Duchess and the mother of three beautiful daughters and her son, William George Arlington, the Viscount Holmes.

RICHARD AND EMILY LIVED COMFORTABLY AT ROSINGS with their children. Richard's dreams of his happy marriage to Emily and being surrounded by laughing children became a reality. They were happy to be the parents of five fine sons. Richard began to realize that he was wrong when he told Emily all those years ago that Rosings was too big by half. With five growing boys, tutors, and nannies, he was often hard-pressed to find an unoccupied room for some peace and quiet. He was so happy and there was nothing he wished to change about his life. Over time, Emily's parents, Mr. and Mrs. Carter, came to accept Richard as *tolerable enough* for their daughter which made their semi-annual visits to Rosings bearable.

~

Caroline and Peter Carter were very happy living together in the parsonage in Kympton. They doted on their children; a boy and a girl. When Peter's parents came to Derbyshire, they were happy to pamper their grandchildren and lavish them with gifts. Even after his marriage, Mrs. Carter continued to order new clothes for her son from the best tailor in London. Caroline was often overheard telling their visitors, *"I never thought I could be happy living in the country all year, but Mr. Carter swept me off my feet. After I met him, I knew there could never be anyone else for me."* Years later, everyone who had ever met Caroline before her marriage, was still shaking their heads in disbelief.

~

Jane and Charles Bingley remained at Birchwood Manor with their four children; two girls and two boys. They were frequent visitors to Pemberley and Kympton; the Darcy children and the Carter children were very close to their Bingley cousins. They all enjoyed the many times summers and holidays were celebrated at Pemberley and Birchwood Manor. Jane and Charles continued to be best friends with Elizabeth and Darcy; they often relied on each other when the challenges and rewards of life called for mutual support.

***

THE HARVEST BALL 1823

Elizabeth was sitting at her dressing table while Hannah pinned her final curls into place. Just as she was finishing, Darcy walked into her room. "I believe I am finished, Mrs. Darcy. Is there anything else I can do for you?"

"Thank you, Hannah. That will be all for now." Her maid curtsied and left the room.

Elizabeth smiled as her husband stood behind her and placed his hands on her shoulders. They looked at their reflections in the glass as Elizabeth covered his hands with her own. "It has already been ten happy years since our first Harvest Ball; so much has happened in that time."

"We hosted our first Harvest Ball when you were almost ready to give birth to Ben; now our boy is almost 10 years old. I remember how badly you wanted to dance that night and I told you that you would have to wait until the following year. I had not wanted our baby to be born in the ballroom. Of course, Alex was born long before the Harvest Ball of 1815." Elizabeth stood to face her husband.

"Yes, I remember that quite well."

"At the rate Ben is growing, he will be taller than me in a few years." Darcy took his wife's hands. "Elizabeth, I am so happy with our life together and our wonderful children. Ben and Alex and then four years ago, our sweet little Frannie Jane. Our lives have been blessed in so many ways and I am so grateful and happy."

"And do not forget that at our first Harvest Ball, Richard met Emily and Peter met Caroline. Georgiana's life was also affected by our Harvest Ball a few years ago."

"Mr. and Mrs. Darcy, matchmakers!" They both laughed.

"We have had a lot to celebrate at each of our Harvest Balls. Now Mr. Darcy, I have a question for you."

"Madame, I am at your service."

"Will you allow me to dance tonight?"

"Why should you not dance?" Darcy looked at his wife and saw the same twinkle in her eyes that he had seen three times before. "Really? You are… another baby?" Elizabeth smiled and nodded at her husband. "Oh, my love, this is the most wonderful news. Are you feeling well?"

"I am well, just the normal sickness in the morning. I saw Mr. Livingston, the new doctor, and he thinks the baby will arrive sometime in March. Another year that we have a good reason not to go to London for the Season!" They both smiled at that thought. "I am glad that Mr. Laurence is enjoying his retirement, but it will be a different experience having someone new helping me bring this baby into the world."

"I am so delighted with your news. I never knew a person could feel so happy and fulfilled every minute of every day and it is all because I had the good sense to marry you."

"*Your* good sense? Once again, you seem to be taking all the credit for our happy marriage. What about *my* good sense?"

"Madam, this topic merits merits discussion, but we must go downstairs to greet our guests. Perhaps we can discuss this matter later this evening."

"That is a very good idea."

As they were descending the stairs, "Oh, and Elizabeth, I prefer that you keep me company tonight and do not dance."

"Yes, master, I shall be happy to obey your command," Elizabeth teased her husband.

"You know I love you very much, Mrs. Darcy."

"Mr. Darcy, your secret is safe with me." Elizabeth and Darcy kissed briefly and then walked to the front door to greet their guests for another Harvest Ball.

~

Richard Charles Darcy arrived in March of 1824 and was the last child born to the Darcys. Elizabeth and Darcy spent every moment they could with their four beautiful children. Every day Elizabeth wore the gold locket Darcy had given her on their first anniversary. It held sketches of all her children and she only took it off when an occasion required more ornate jewelry. The family resided in Derbyshire for most of the year and all their children learned to ride at an early age. Frannie Jane and Alex were talented musicians like their Aunt Georgiana, while Ben and Richard loved to read about history and politics. Elizabeth and Darcy showed their children the small cave that had been a favorite hideout of their Papa and Uncle Richard but their children were clever enough to find their own places to hide. The Darcys continued to hold a Harvest Ball every September and often reminisced about the tumultuous events leading up to the first one. The Harvest Ball of 1813 was followed by many, many years of happiness and love and an ongoing discussion of whether it was Elizabeth or Darcy who had the most good sense to marry the other.

The End

AUTHOR'S NOTE

Thank you for your purchase of New Beginnings Book 2: The Harvest Ball! I am honored that you have chosen to spend some of your valuable time reading my book and I hope you enjoyed it. All the details about the Great Fog of 1813 and the Thames Frost Fair are historically accurate.

Support from buyers like you make it possible for independent authors like me to continue writing. Please consider leaving a review on Amazon. Just a few positive words can make a big difference. Thank you and happy reading!!

I would like to thank everyone in the JAFF community for their continuing support. My undying gratitude to my beta readers: Susan Sandberg, Anna Moskau and Patricia Alden. Their suggestions, support and love are invaluable to me. To Mr.

McGurk – thank you for your continuous encouragement and always being there for me. I love you to the moon and back!

ALSO BY LILY BERNARD:

An Invisible Thread

New Beginnings Book 1: Wickham's Revenge

Coming in September: Mr. Darcy's Destiny

Work in Progress: Willoughby: A Sense and Sensibility Mystery

Author's Bio:

Lily Bernard grew up in the desert southwest and now resides in the land of sunshine and palm trees. She fell in love with Jane Austen many years ago and discovered JAFF at a time in her life when a HEA was very important. Lily is a retired speech pathologist who loves to travel, cook, spend time with her family and friends, and read, especially anything related to Jane Austen.

Made in the USA
Middletown, DE
30 November 2023